THE KNOCK-KNEED COWBOY
A TALE OF BEING "JUST RIGHT"...JUST AS WE ARE

WRITTEN & ILLUSTRATED BY
BILLIE WILLMON JENKIN

This book is a work of fiction. Names, characters, places, and incidents are either products of the author's imagination or, if real, are used fictitiously. No horses, frogs, dogs, cattle, humanoids—or any other species—were harmed in the writing of this book.

The Knock-Kneed Cowboy:
A Tale of Being "Just Right"... Just As We Are

Written and illustrated by Billie Willmon Jenkin

Published by
Empowering For Change,
a division of JENKINTERNATIONAL CORPORATION

www.knock-kneedcowboy.com
www.empoweringforchange.com

©2009 Billie Willmon Jenkin

ISBN 978-0-6152-2596-8
LCCN 2008909825

All rights reserved. No part of this book may be reproduced or transmitted in any form or by any means, electronic or mechanical, including photocopying, recording or by any information storage and retrieval system, without written permission from the author, except for the inclusion of brief quotations in a review. For information, contact knock.kneed.cowboy@gmail.com

Self-Acceptance

This book contains interwoven stories, to be appreciated at various levels of understanding. The original story was invented for my sons' entertainment on a long trip from our west Texas ranch to a family visit in Houston. At first it was simply a magical, feel-good story about a cowboy who got his wish to be bow-legged like his peers.

In time, my recognition of the need for self-acceptance in our society called for an "upgrade" in plot and theme. Consequently, the outside story centers on Honey, a girl who is unhappy about her height. Just as easily, this character could be a boy who is upset that he is shorter or less muscular than his peers.

Honey's appreciation of herself is intended as a gift for everyone—regardless of age, gender, body shape, or any other variable. As parents, teachers, or other adults, we can nurture self-appreciation—or starve it—with our attitudes toward youngsters. For that reason, this book is one for the entire family—or classroom.

Table of Contents

Chapter		Page number
1	The Class Picture	7
2	Grandpa Introduces Casey	15
3	Be Careful What You Wish For	19
4	Troubles with Beans	25
5	Troubles to the Rescue	31
6	A Promising Start	35
7	A Change of Plans	39
8	Attention on Florence	45
9	Wannabe Heroes	51
10	Drama at the Ice Cream Parlor	59
11	Casey's Head Spins	65
12	The Womanly Art of Rescue	75
13	Casey's Visitors	81
14	Mr. Warren Steps Up	85
15	Hospital Visitors	89
16	Casey's Big Decision	95
17	Honey's Lesson	99
18	The Family Trees	103
	Creative Corral	111
	Uncommon Horse Sense	117
	Gracias, Pardner!	119
	The Author	121
	Fans of *The Knock-Kneed Cowboy*	123

"No one can make you feel inferior without your consent."

—Eleanor Roosevelt
Wife of Franklin D. Roosevelt, 32nd US president
First Lady of the United States 1933–1945
1884–1962

Chapter 1

The Class Picture

It was a sunny Saturday in this part of west Texas when Honey awoke. She slipped on a shirt, her favorite pair of Wranglers[1] and her well-worn boots. Remembering the chill in the air, she grabbed her 4-H[2] jacket at the last moment and hurried downstairs. Quickly, she fed and watered the French Lops.[3] Honey had selected these unusual rabbits as a 4-H project this year.

Usually she would enjoy spending the morning petting and caring for her rabbits, but today Honey was going to visit Grandpa for a few hours. Grandpa lived in a cozy house on a small ranch. This ranch was near the edge of the tiny town where her mother had been raised. Honey had never known her grandmother, who died when Honey was a baby. But Grandpa went out of his way to be more than twice the grandparent most girls had.

When Grandpa knew she was coming, he always baked biscuits. He would put the dough in a covered heavy iron "Dutch oven" and set it into glowing coals, like cowboys did on cattle drives. The biscuits, dripping with fresh-churned

---

1 Wrangler is a favorite brand of jeans throughout the Unites States, but especially popular among the cowboys in Texas and the rest of the Southwest. See *www.wrangler.com*
2 4-H is a nationwide organization that teaches skills and develops confidence. It is especially popular in rural areas. See: *www.4-h.org/*
3 French Lops are large rabbits with long droopy ears that make them look like basset hounds in fur.

butter, were proof of her grandfather's love. Honey's favorite drink was the ice-cold tea, brewed by the sun in the gallon-sized pickle jar. She loved to chill the tea with the ice Grandpa chipped using his old ice pick.

A slow-cooked dish Grandpa called "Cowboy Beans"—with more home-grown beef than beans—was her all-time favorite dish. If Grandpa had been a cowboy camp cook, he had never "'fessed up." But his stories of the "olden days" and cowboy ways showed he was for real. Those stories—according to Grandpa "absolutely true"—contained messages that made Honey's life happier.

Today Honey really needed one of Grandpa's stories. It had been a tough week at school, ever since the class group pictures had been handed out. Spending time with Grandpa was much better than spending her time alone, thinking about the incident and about herself.

Even before she got her own copy of the group photo, she heard Charley, the boy she had a crush on, make a joke: "Look at Honey! She looks just like that old scarecrow Dad puts in the cornfield to keep the crows away. Hey, Honey, want a job this summer?"

She couldn't decide which was worse: Charley making fun of her height, or her classmates laughing at Charley's joke. Seeing the picture with her own eyes really hurt. She understood why the others laughed. There she was on the back row, a head taller than anyone else in the fifth-grade class! She was even taller than Terrible Tom, the class clown!

After hearing Charley's words and seeing the class photo, Honey had scooted down in her seat. She wanted to disappear, or at least become a lot shorter. The rest of the week at school, she tried to look as small as possible, slumping over even when she stood up.

This morning, though, was a break from a hard week. Honey and her four-footed pal, a fuzzy pooch called Snickers, walked to Grandpa's house. It was a short walk from "downtown," where Honey's mother Suze had stopped to shop. The townsfolk thought her grandfather lived in the country; the ranchers thought Grandpa's home was in town.

Sandy Gulch, Texas, was really a community rather than a town. It was where Grandpa and Grandma had moved when they married. This was where Suze had grown up, and where Honey felt as at home as in her own back yard. She loved the old stores, the friendliness of the people, and how everything and everybody seemed to "belong." She knew there was a lot of history in and around Sandy Gulch. One day she would ask Grandpa to tell her all about it.

Her own spirits lifted as she and Snickers neared Grandpa's place. It would be good to spend a few hours with Grandpa, the only two-legged being in the world who understood Honey's feelings. Snickers jogged and jiggled with joy, as if she, too, looked forward to seeing Grandpa.

Honey and Snickers felt even happier as they reached Grandpa's squeaky-hinged gate. From his porch, Grandpa looked like his same old friendly self, only shorter. *Oh, no! Am I even taller than Grandpa?* Honey wondered.

Snickers displayed her best tail-wagging and body-wiggling efforts when she saw Grandpa. Honey put on a smile, and continued practicing making herself look shorter. As Grandpa hobbled to meet them, Honey noticed the flicker of a question in his face.

Maybe Grandpa's questioning look was just her imagination. Soon she saw only the smile of his love for her. His friendly arms reached around her for the hug they always shared. His stubbly chin beard brushed her cheek gently as he planted a kiss.

Snickers, still showing off her best wiggles, was rewarded with one of Grandpa's best-ever ear scratches *and* a nibble of something Grandpa called "canine candy." After petting Snickers, Grandpa straightened and looked at his granddaughter.

Smiling from his heart, he remarked, "My gracious, Honey! It's great to see you! Say, looks like you 'grew-some'," Grandpa chuckled, as he did when he played with words.

Usually Honey would laugh along with Grandpa's word-play. But right now, she felt *gruesome* that she had grown even a little! "Yeah, Grandpa. I'm 'fraid I've grown a *lot*," she answered, slumping even more than before. "I wish I were short like Melissa. All the boys in class like her."

"And you think they like her because she's short and don't like you because you're tall. Is that it?" Grandpa asked.

"Yes, Sir. Seems to me like that's the way it is," Honey responded politely to her grandfather. Saying "Sir" and "Ma'am," "please," and "thank you" was a habit her parents—and Grandpa—had instilled in her since she was little. It sounded unusual nowadays, even in rural west Texas.

"I'm not sayin'[4] you're wrong, young lady. I *am* sayin' that we often get from people what we think we're gonna get, what folks call a 'self-fulfillin' prophecy,'" Grandpa countered. "But we can talk about this over some lunch. Could I interest ya in some beans-n-cornbread with a big ol' goblet of iced tea?" he asked. Looking at Snickers, he added, "And maybe some doggy biscuits?"

Honey enjoyed the familiar surroundings as she stepped into Grandpa's house. In one corner stood the old coat rack made from a mesquite tree that he had chopped down when he and Grandma had first married. On one of the branches hung a much-worn denim jacket; on another, a dusty cowboy hat that had once been black. The old rack even held a rope Grandpa had used years ago when he was still a working cowboy. Honey imagined she could smell the leather of the old saddle and cowboy boots left in another corner.

On the mantle above the fireplace stood the same pictures she'd always remembered. Her favorite was one of Grandpa and Grandma Flo sitting, holding Honey before she was old enough to stand up by herself. She remembered Grandpa saying that the picture had been taken just a few weeks before Grandma died. Funny, Honey realized, she had never noticed that Grandma Flo looked taller than Grandpa.

The familiar, mouth-watering aromas came from the kitchen. Without words, Grandpa and Honey began the familiar routine of serving lunch: Grandpa dished up the fresh-churned butter, the beefy beans, and today's special treat: hot homemade "cowboy cornbread." Honey quickly

---

4   sayin' = saying. Although Texans *can* pronounce –*ing* words (like *saying* and *fulfilling*), they often drop the final *g* sound, especially when speaking informally. Other sounds are also dropped as they speak. Most English-speakers, however, can translate most "Texanisms."

filled their goblets with the hand-chipped ice and fresh-brewed sun tea. Snickers danced like a ballerina while Grandpa poured bacon drippings over a cold crumbled biscuit and set it in her dish beside the table.

When Grandpa and Honey first sat down to their meal, the only sounds were those of the few cattle near the house and of Snickers licking her bowl clean. Honey stayed bent over her food, her honey-colored bangs hiding her eyes. After a few bites of food, Grandpa cleared his throat.

"Now what's this about being too tall, Honey?" Grandpa asked with a relaxed tone. Honey didn't respond right away. When she did look up from her food, Grandpa could see that she was ready to cry.

"Oh, Grandpa! I *hate* being so tall! I'm taller even than most of the *sixth*-grade boys! I know it probably doesn't make much sense to you, but I just want to be short like the popular girls are," she said, tears spilling from Honey's eyes.

"Honey, I can understand your feelings. In fact, if you like, I'll tell you about a guy who could *really* make sense out of what you're saying," Grandpa answered gently. "Would you like to hear about someone who went through something like you?"

"Sure, Grandpa. Your stories always make me feel better," Honey replied. After they chatted a few more minutes, Honey took the dishes to the sink to wash them. She knew that the food on the plates would become hard as concrete if today's story was as long as most of Grandpa's tales.

Dishes dried and put away, Grandpa and Honey went to the front room. Snickers joined them and immediately rolled onto her back, eager for her fat tummy to be scratched. Settling into his favorite chair, Grandpa (pretending not to remember what they had planned), scratched his head and asked, "Now, what were we going to do?"

Playing along with Grandpa's game, Honey grinned mischievously, "I think you said we would go to town and get some ice cream!"

Chapter 2

Grandpa Introduces Casey

"Well, matter of fact, I *have* been thinkin' that ice cream would make excellent dessert. But first—oh, yes, now I remember—I have a true story about a guy who wasn't very happy with his body, either," Grandpa said as an introduction to his tale.

> **Years ago in the far, far edges of the wild Wild West, lived a cowboy named Casey. Casey could break any bronc and manage any maverick. As a courteous, courageous cowboy of the wild Wild West, he did dangerous and difficult deeds.[5]**

Honey could tell by the way this tale was starting out that it was going to take a while. So, she got comfortable and patted the sofa to invite Snickers to join her. Then she focused on the story that Grandpa claimed to be one hundred percent true.

---

5   Grandpa's story, which happens long ago, is indented and in a different font (type of print) and a different color. No quotation marks are used, unless someone besides Grandpa is speaking.

This same Casey—tanned and talented—was liked by the ladies and admired by the men. In fact, only one feature kept Casey from feelin' completely content: his legs. Casey envied the magnificent bend in the legs of the many manly men of the wild Wild West. It looked like these manly men had spent their lives with legs wrapped around a fine, fat steed.

Casey, however, seemed to be cursed with knees that knocked together as he walked. He imagined that everyone heard his knees bump-bump-bumping together when he strode down the street. *"Clattering Casey" is what they call me,* he thought. *Whoever heard of a knock-kneed cowboy?*

> **Scarcely a day passed that Casey didn't fret about his knocking knees. "Why can't I look like a real cowboy?" Casey sighed. "I would give my favorite horse to have legs like the other cowboys."**

Grandpa took a brief break from his story, pretending to swat a fly while checking to see if Honey was still listening. Snickers still lay unmoving, belly side up, asleep with her feet in the air. Honey, knowing the story was far from over, looked up to find out why Grandpa had suddenly gone silent.

Satisfied that half his audience was still awake, Grandpa continued.

> **Early one morning, Casey rose and made his cowboy breakfast. He enjoyed his boiled "branchwater" coffee. It was hot, black, strong, and full of coffee grounds. Fat slabs of hog meat, which city folks call bacon, sizzled in the iron skillet. Biscuits, left over from the day before, completed his meal. The cowhound Troubles, Casey's constant companion, lived up to his name. As usual, Troubles sauntered by to beg for his share of the "fixin's," as cowboys call a prepared meal.**

> **Obligingly, Casey tossed half a rock-hard biscuit to Troubles. The pooch scarfed it down with one huge "GULP!" then begged for more. Next, the cowboy shared the hog meat. Still hungry, the hound howled until Casey gave him a huge pot of beans left on the stove overnight. As soon as the pot of beans was within his reach, the greedy hound quaffed the bean juice. Then he lapped up the beans. If a dog could burp, Casey's big scare would never have occurred.**

After breakfast, Casey readied himself and his horse Horace to ride the rough range of the wild Wild West. Just as they started off, Troubles ran ahead of the cowboy and his fine steed. Trying to lead the group, Troubles ran right between Horace's front feet, causin' the poor horse to stumble.

At that point, Casey seriously thought about sending Troubles back to the house. But seein' the dog's apologetic expression, Casey believed Troubles would soon settle down. So, the cowboy, his horse and dog headed out to ride the range of the wild Wild West. They would find the mavericks that had strayed from the herd.

Cattle aren't the brightest of creatures, but Casey felt comfortable workin' with them. It was going to be a long, hot day. In the heat they would need to travel slowly. Travelin' too fast in this weather would cause heat exhaustion or even sunstroke. Casey had heard of cowboys who took their day's work too seriously and who were heard talkin' "out of their head." No, he valued his sanity and health too much to rush today.

Honey, not sure that Grandpa's tale was "going anywhere," shifted on the couch. She looked up to see if Grandpa's eyes had that far-away look that showed his mind was stuck in another time and place. Unsure, she declared, "Grandpa, this is a neat story, but I don't see what it's got to do with me being too tall."

Chapter 3

Be Careful What You Wish For

"Don't worry your pretty head about what I'm gettin' at. In the end, you'll understand how this applies. Now, how 'bout you just relax and enjoy the story. After all, it *is* one hundred percent true," Grandpa added with a twinkle in his eye.

"Okey-dokey, Grandpa. You never disappoint me with your stories. I'm sure your story will make sense *some day*," Honey joked, with a grin that let Grandpa know she really *was* enjoying the tale.

After a few hours of ridin' the range of the wild Wild West, Casey stopped at a shallow creek to rest and to water his favorite horse - Horace. Troubles had disappeared, likely chasin' rabbits. Seeing his own knock-kneed reflection in the water, Casey moaned miserably, "I would give my back teeth just to have bowed legs like the other cowboys!"

"Be careful what you wish for; you just might get it!" croaked a voice nearby.

Casey whirled around and quickly drew his pistol to defend himself against an unknown enemy.

To his surprise, no one was there.

I must have imagined it, thought Casey. *The sun must have baked my brain already.*

As the thirsty Horace continued to drink, Casey's thoughts returned to his legs. "My legs look like scissors," he said. "Oh, how I wish that they were bowed like those of the other cowpokes!"

"I told you that you need to be careful what you wish for," the croaky voice again warned.

I know I'm not crazy, Casey thought to himself, beginning to look low and high for the source of the voice. "Where are you? Who are you?" Casey asked, still searchin'.

"I'm right down here by your foot," the croaker replied, "and you may call me Gus."

Continuin' to search, Casey could find no suitable source of such human-sounding communication. "WHERE?" the cowboy again inquired.

"Right HERE!" Gus replied in the loudest voice his little lungs could produce.

Checkin' that nobody was around who might witness his strange actions, Casey knelt low to the ground to find what had made the sound. Nearby he found the only other living creature—a very ordinary-looking frog—which was balanced lazily on the muddy edge of the creek. "Surely not you!" the cowboy sputtered in a bewildered tone.

"And just why not?" the frog retorted. "Why do you human beings think that you're the only creatures with any sense?"

"Why... well... it's just...," Casey's voice trailed off, as Horace gazed questioningly at the man who had, until this point, seemed quite sane. "...Well, who are you, REALLY?"

"As I said, just call me Gus. I happen to be your fairy godfrog," the gallant Gus gasped.

"Uh-HUH!" Casey chuckled, "and I am Cinderella! First of all, I don't believe in fairies, especially froggy fairies. But if I did, I wouldn't believe in you. Everybody knows that if there really were such things as fairies, they would have wings and wands. And I don't see a sign of either one on you!"

"Now, just how long do you think I'd last if I had wings?" Gus retorted. "Every Tom, Dick, and Mary would pick me up, rub me, and make a wish! Pretty soon I wouldn't have any skin at all, and everybody else would have warts! Either that or someone would pick me up and take me home, putting me in an old box. Then my smooth skin would dry up, and I'd look like an old toad and have to be someone's slave. No thanks; I'd rather look quite ordinary!"

"Okay, okay. Maybe you really are a fairy godfrog," Casey continued. "So, can you get me my bowed legs?"

"Look," explained Gus with all the patience he could muster, "it's like I was telling you before: You have to be careful what you wish for. You just might get it. Besides, I wasn't sent here to be your slave, but to help keep you out of trouble. And I'm telling you that you need to think again about what you're wishing for."

"Just what does a frog know about what human beings want and need?" the discontented cowpuncher complained. "Never mind your silly warning. I WANT TO HAVE LEGS THAT LOOK LIKE THE OTHER COWBOYS' LEGS!!"

"You asked for it; just remember that I tried to warn you!" Gus grumbled, as he vanished below the surface of the pond.

Completely taken in by Grandpa's story, Honey leaned forward to catch every word. She didn't want to admit that fairy godfrogs *might* really exist, and she still couldn't understand why Grandpa was telling *this* story. But she loved the excitement in his voice and could hardly wait to hear how Casey was going to get his wish.

"Yee-HAA!" Casey exclaimed in celebration. "I'm gonna have legs like everybody else's!" Dancin' like a wind-up toy, with his knees clatterin' and keepin' time, Casey looked ecstatic, but crazy.

Startled by Casey's yells and cavortin', Horace suddenly raised his head to see what was going on. Troubles, hearing the shouts, came dartin' out from his rabbit chase to rescue his master. He stopped at a distance when he saw his master jumpin' up and down and heard the loud clatterin' sound.

"Sorry, ole boys!" said Casey, controllin' himself. "I didn't mean to scare you. By the way, Horace, Troubles, you better take one last look at these scissor-legs of mine. Pretty soon, I'm gonna to have the most cowboy-lookin' legs you or anybody else ever saw!"

Troubles cocked his head to one side, like dogs do when they're trying to figure out a strange sound. Realizin' his master was safe, even if he was a bit crazy, the mutt sauntered off into the bushes, ready to explore again.

Water drippin' from Horace's mouth disturbed the smooth surface of the creek. Suddenly Casey caught a glorious reflection of himself. There in the rippled reflection was the image he had dreamed about: a tanned and talented cowboy with bowed legs—not as tall as he had once appeared, but a bona fide, bronzed, bow-legged cowboy!

What joy this image brought to Casey! He whistled happily and found himself thinkin' about the incident with Gus. Had Casey simply imagined a promise? Was he truly goin' to have real-cowboy legs? Or would he always be the brunt of cowboys' cruel jokes?

"Grandpa, I thought you were going to tell me a *true story*," Honey reminded him with a bit of a whine. Why did you change your mind and start telling me fairy tales?"

"Now, Honey, it's a well-known fact that truth is stranger than fiction. I want to be sure this story isn't *too* strange." Not sure what Grandpa was saying about truth and fiction, she let his comments pass so he could get on with his story.

Chapter 4

Troubles with Beans

Seeing that Honey was ready to listen again, Grandpa took up where his story had left off.

As Casey mounted up, Troubles reappeared, ready to check out the last herd of cattle for the day. Gazin' into the distance, Casey saw three figures on horseback. How lithe the men looked with their legs loungin' lazily around the bulging bellies of their stately steeds! He compared their legs to his own lower limbs and the knock knees which forced his legs straight out, almost at right angles to his horse's legs.

What a foolish spectacle he was! To himself, Casey looked more like a rodeo clown than a true cowboy. Gus's promise momentarily forgotten, Casey sighed forlornly and spurred Horace to a higher gear. Still loping lazily, Horace managed to close the gap between them and the waiting bow-legged cowboys.

"Howdy, pardner!" one of the cattlemen shouted as Casey appeared. "Good to see y'all ag'in! Say, I do declare that horse of yore's gets skinnier and that hound of yore's gets fatter every time I see you. If you don't quit feedin' that mutt, I swear he's gonna explode! In fact, he came up to our camp a while ago and whined until we gave him the last of the beans we had.

"But you look just the same! I swear: you never change at all!" Casey imagined a smirk with the last comment. Were these guys poking fun at his legs?

Casey quickly glanced down at his own legs, which looked like tree limbs sproutin' from the saddle. He wished they'd at least hang straight down. "Yep, men," replied Casey with a small smile. "It's great to see y'all too. I haven't seen y'all since forever." Troubles, bored with sittin' still while cowboys blathered about nothin', had disappeared down another rabbit trail.

"Say, we've got a round-up startin' tomorrow, helpin' Old Man Warren, out on the *Rockin' W*. How 'bout if y'all join us about mid-mornin'?" the slender cowpoke invited.

"Sounds like a plan," Casey agreed. "I've got one more pasture to check out today, but I'll figger on seein' y'all in th' mornin'. The usual meeting place?"

"Yep, the Chuck Wagon Cafe," answered another bow-legged cowboy.

With that, Casey turned Horace toward the shortcut to the pasture: a rocky ledge that led to the cattle's favorite grazing spot. As the sun started sinking and the heat faded, Casey began feeling uneasy.

The countryside changed before him: the rocks appeared sharper and the slope more extreme than earlier. Startin' down the slope toward a steep ridge, Casey noticed the gnarled shrubs that grew out at strange angles from the rocky terrain. Sharp shadows crossin' the path gave Casey an eerie feelin'. When a jackrabbit leapt across a path, Horace himself seemed jittery— not a good sign in the animal on which Casey's life depended.

Ghostly shadows, narrowing trails, and Horace's skittishness combined to make the late afternoon ride frightenin'. Sometimes Troubles trotted along with Casey and Horace. Others times he disappeared to check out the rabbit situation or to relieve himself of the beans he had enjoyed for breakfast and lunch.

"Whoa, boy!!" Casey called to Horace as the path grew still steeper and narrower. Horace slowed down, picking the way carefully between large boulders and along the narrow, slippery passage.

Troubles—experienced cowhound that he was—realized that his trail skills were needed to lead this dangerous situation. With no room to spare, he darted suddenly from behind the aging cayuse. Just as he reached the front, his beanpile exploded deafeningly near poor old Horace's head.

Whether the thud of the explosion or the stench of the fermented beans caused the horse to spook, no one ever knew. Immediately, however, Horace whinnied fearfully and reared, front hooves pawing the air and back hooves skidding along loose rock. Horse and rider tumbled off the ledge.

Everything happened so fast that Casey could think of only one thing: Hang on tight! His feet stayed in the stirrups, one hand on the saddle horn, and one on the reins. As Horace and Casey plunged down the cliff, Casey's boot, splayed out far to the side, caught in a shrub, slowed the fall, but spun them around. Horace's body slammed

into a rocky ledge and trapped Casey's other leg between the horse and the narrow shelf which held them.

Casey's howl of pain roused Horace, who struggled to regain his footin' on the precarious precipice. One hoof at a time, he managed to get his balance enough to release most of his weight from Casey's trapped leg. As Horace finally found a foothold for his fourth hoof, Casey shifted his own weight.

Unfortunately, the shift spoiled their delicate balance.

Once again, the ground raced up to meet them as they plunged downward, spiralin' through space, bouncin' through brush, and slidin' down the slippery slope until the ground leveled. Both man and horse lay completely still.

In her mind Honey could see the accident just as Grandpa described it. "Did Casey and Horace *both* get killed, Grandpa?" she asked fearfully.

"To wish you were someone else is to waste the person you are."

—Author unknown

Chapter 5

Troubles to the Rescue

Grandpa grinned slowly and said, "If they *did* survive, whatcha bet they put Troubles out of their misery?"

"Out of whose misery, Grandpa?" Honey asked, confused.

"Out of Casey's and Horace's misery. The problems Troubles causes are always someone else's."

Meantime, hearing the slidin' rocks, Troubles whirled around to check out the noise. Shocked that he could no longer see his master and the old horse on the trail, he sniffed around the area, hoping his eyes were playin' a trick on him. When even his trusty nose couldn't find his master, Troubles—sniffin' and howlin' all the way—raced back up the steep slope to get a better view.

Hearing Horace's whinnyin' and Casey's moaning, Troubles realized that they both needed his help. The cowboys who had so generously fed Troubles their leftover beans were long gone. So it was up to the heroic hound himself to rescue his master and the fine steed.

Troubles loved Casey with all his doggy heart, but never considered his master the most skilled rider in the world. It was really a good thing that he—Troubles the Terrific—was around to rescue his good—but not very bright—friends.

Look at what miracles I create by being here to save Master and Horse! Troubles thought as he rounded the last rock and saw both Horace and Casey startin' to stand up all by themselves. *Because I have rescued them, they will love me more than ever. It feels great to be INCOMPARABLE CATTLE CANINE!*

Casey's and Horace's greetings, however, were not quite as welcomin' as Troubles had expected. As soon as Casey saw him, he bent over, picked up a rock, and threw it at Troubles. The rock caught the hound solidly on his head. Astounded by his master's reaction, Troubles turned to run from the crazed cowboy.

But the pooch wasn't quite fast enough. Horace laid his ears flat and, like an angry bull, charged at Troubles. Catching the confused mutt, the usually-gentle Horace lowered his head below Troubles' belly. Then with a mighty upward thrust, Horace sent the mutt flyin' through the air!

Hitting the dirt, Troubles shook off the confusion and the dust. *Wow! What kind of appreciation is that for all my dedicated service?* Troubles wondered. *Both those guys must have had some blows to the head. See if I ever rescue them again!* Concerned that Horace and Casey might cause him real harm, Troubles quickly headed down a different path from the loco horse and rider.

Coming home sore from bouncin' down the cliff—and from the sudden stop—Casey unsaddled Horace and settled in for a quiet evenin'. Too tired to eat supper, he tried to read. The excitement from the day, however, seemed to stop his concentration.

I wonder if Gus really meant it when said, "You asked for it," Casey began ponderin'. *If Gus really is my fairy godfrog, then tomorrow I'll surely awaken with the legs of my dreams. In fact, if I go to sleep now, it will be mornin' before I know it. Whoopee!*

As if he had finally convinced himself that his fairy godfrog was real, with a smile on his lips, the cowboy closed his eyelids. *When I wake up,* he reminded himself, *I'll have those bowed legs I've dreamed of. Won't my new legs surprise those other cowboys at the Chuck Wagon Cafe in the mornin'? No more makin' fun of my knock knees!*

With those hopeful thoughts, Casey drifted off into Dreamland, awaitin' the sunrise and his handsome new silhouette.

"Most people are about as happy as they make up their minds to be."

—Abraham Lincoln
Sixteenth President of the United States
February 12, 1809–April 15, 1865

Chapter 6

A Promising Start

When Snickers stood and stretched, Honey took the opportunity to do the same. Then she returned to the sofa to hear Grandpa continue his story.

> The next morning the sun rose brightly, shining into Casey's window and into his eyes. Troubles, hungry for "fixin's" cautiously whined softly just inside the torn screen door. Casey, guilty over his actions yesterday, rolled over and apologetically said to the cowdog, "It's okay, ol' boy. I'm not going to hurt you. Come on in."
>
> Delighted by his master's tone, the eager Troubles bounded onto the bed, washing the cowboy's face with sloppy, stinky kisses. Preferring not to have his face smell like a dog's breath, Casey sat up, squintin' against the brilliant light. Rubbin' his eyes, he suddenly realized that this was his special day—better than a birthday or a vacation or even his favorite holiday. This was the day his dream had come true! This was the day he got his real-cowboy legs!
>
> Enthusiastically, Casey threw back the covers to admire his new form. As he blinked his eyes against the sun, he could scarcely believe what he saw! His first reaction was, "I'm surely dreamin'!

I'd better pinch myself to be sure that I'm really awake!" Sure enough, what he saw was true.

There, freed from the bed covers, were the same two knock-kneed legs that he had cursed all his life!

"That fibbing frog! That terrible toad! That goldarned Gus! Why did he tell me I'd get new legs? I'll never trust another frog as long as I live! They are all liars! Fairy godfrog, indeed!" Casey ranted, sendin' the slobberin' Troubles sailin' out of bed and sprawlin' onto the floor. Troubles, rememberin' yesterday's tirade and the sore spot where Casey's rock had caught him, raced out of the shack in fear.

Casey, alone with his thoughts of disappointment, got out of bed, miserable. Soon, the growlin' in Troubles' stomach overcame his fear. Cautiously, he skulked inside, and sat beside the door pretendin' to be invisible. After Troubles was sure that Casey had returned to his usual grumpy mornin' self, the dog began beggin' for his breakfast.

Still frustrated over his unchanged legs, Casey hurled a cold biscuit to him, hopin' to be left in silence. The hard biscuit grazed the hound's already-wounded left ear. Yelpin' in pain and fear, Troubles quickly grabbed the biscuit and then scooted under a chair, waitin' for his master to calm down.

In the portion of the room he called his kitchen, Casey filled a coffeepot with water and set it on the small propane stove to boil. Next, he warmed some bacon drippings on the same stove.

Soon after he had poured the warm drippings over the biscuit bits and set them down for the now-more-patient Troubles, his coffee water began to boil. Casey stirred-in two handfuls of coffee grounds, making sure the coffee would be super-strong.

Then, as he'd learned from cowboys before him, he threw some crushed eggshells into the thick mixture, causing the coffee grounds to sink to the bottom of the pot. As the grounds were separating, he searched the cabin for his cleanest dirty cup. Having wiped out the residue from yesterday's brew, he poured in the steaming, dark mixture.

After the ritual, he sat down on the side of the bed and sipped his coffee, plannin' the day ahead. It seemed strange to him to be meeting at the cafe in the middle of the mornin'. In years past, cowboys would pack the supplies the night before, and meet on the range with their gear by this time of day. They certainly wouldn't have met in a cafe mid-mornin' to begin their day's work.

He gathered the needed items, refilled his mug with the inky brew, then headed out the door to saddle Horace. As Casey stepped into the sunlight, something magical happened to his attitude: He suddenly knew that Gus's promise would be fulfilled today.

Casey was so excited about what the day would hold that he seemed to forget the problems Troubles caused yesterday. "C'mon, ol' boy," he sang out. "We're gonna have some fun today!"

Chapter 7

A Change of Plans

"What do you think, Honey? Is Casey going to get those cowboy legs today?" Grandpa asked.

"You're trying to find out if I believe in fairy godfrogs, aren't you, Grandpa?" Honey replied, smoothly avoiding the question. "Besides, Casey keeps talkin' like Gus *promised* him something. I didn't hear Gus promise anything. It sounded more like a *warning* to me," Honey pointed out.

"I guess we're gonna find out, aren't we?" Grandpa's blue eyes twinkled with a teasing grin.

> When Casey, Horace, and Troubles reached the Chuck Wagon Cafe, only one of the bowlegged cowboys was present. "Howdy, Billy Bob. Good to see you. Are the others still sleepin' in?" Casey asked the worried-looking cowhand.
>
> "Naw," Billy Bob replied. "They been gone awhile, but they wanted me to stay here so ya wouldn't think we'd all run off without ya. There's been a kind of emergency out on the *Rockin' W* ranch. If yer ready, I'll pay up and explain everything on the way out to the *W*." The cowboy rose and left a few coins on the table; then they both mounted their horses and left for the ranch.

On the way to the *Rockin' W*, Billy Bob explained to Casey what was happening. "It's like this," Billy Bob began. "You know Old Man Warren, don't ya?"

"I guess you mean Amos Warren?" Casey clarified.

"That's the one," Billy Bob answered. "The really old guy passed away a few years ago. I guess Amos is not very old. I just got in the habit of sayin' 'Old Man'. Not too respectful, I s'pose."

Casey glanced at Billy Bob and, with his eyes, agreed about the disrespect. Then, Billy Bob continued with his story. "Well, anyway, Mr. Warren has a couple of kids, both girls. The youngest one—Rebecca, or I think they call her Becky—is the one whose mama dog got bitten by a nest of rattlesnakes some time back."

"I think I remember that," Casey answered. "Wasn't the little girl standin' right there when it happened?"

"That's right," Billy Bob confirmed. "That mama dog had been in the family since the little girl was a baby. That little girl—so I'm told—would climb up on that dog's back even before she learned to walk. And that dog would walk around the house with the little girl hanging on, arms and legs wrapped around the dog's neck and stomach."

Casey smiled, imaginin' what a toddler would look like ridin' a dog. Then Billy Bob continued. "When the little girl saw her best friend die, she cried for hours on end. The grown-ups thought they were gonna have to take her to the doctor to get her settled down.

"But then, the girl's big sister came and talked to her. You see, the mama dog had a brand-new litter of puppies, just a few days old. They didn't even have their eyes open yet," Billy Bob explained.

"What I found out today is that the older girl—Florence, I think she's called—had comforted the little sister by telling her that the mama dog was countin' on the two of them to take care of the puppies since she couldn't. And, Florence had said, Becky could have the pick of the litter for her own," said Billy Bob.

"I hear the little girl went immediately to the smallest of the puppies, the one that looked most like the mama dog. As it turned out," the cowboy explained to Casey, "that was the perfect choice."

"What do you mean by 'the perfect choice'?" asked Casey. "Isn't one puppy just as good as the other?"

"Well, maybe that's true, usually," Billy Bob answered, "but not this time. Those two girls fed those puppies by hand. They'd get up in the middle of the night and feed them with Becky's doll bottles. Later, they taught the pups to drink milk from a bowl. Next, they started mixing a little baby cereal in the milk, gradually getting the puppies used to solid food."

"So I still don't see why the littlest puppy was the best choice for Becky," Casey commented. "And what's this got to do with us makin' this trip out to the *Rockin' W*?"

"I'm tryin' to explain as fast as I can," Billy Bob drawled, irritated. "Those two girls worked night and day feedin' the puppies; but after a couple of weeks, the only puppy left was the one Becky had chosen for herself.

"So, what I'm tryin' to get to is that the little girl got even more attached to this puppy than she had to its mama. It's kinda like she felt that the puppy was her baby, her havin' raised it and all. Early this mornin' when she and the pup were out and about, it fell into an old cave."

"You mean to tell me that we're not goin' on a cattle drive? We're goin' to rescue a dog?" Casey bellowed. "How about if I told the little girl she could have my dog?" he added, glaring down at Troubles, who was keeping well out of the reach of Horace's feet and head.

"I don't understand you, Casey! Have you got a rock for a heart?" Billy Bob scowled at Casey like he thought Casey might well be the lowest form of human life—and maybe even non-human life. "That little girl loves that puppy as much as most folks love their mama or their kids! How is it you think that worthless mutt of yours is gonna make her feel happy? Everybody knows your dog; there's a reason he's called Troubles."

Troubles, hearing his name, came to collect more praise, trotting immediately in front of the two riders. Startled by the sudden movement, Billy Bob's horse half-reared, jolting the cowboy into even more irritation. "See what I mean, Casey? Your dog is less than worthless. No wonder you're so hard-hearted about dogs!

"How 'bout you just forget about this mutt, and let's go rescue the little girl's puppy? I don't think she can take any more loss right now." Casey could tell by Billy Bob's tone that the rest of the ride to the *Rockin' W* would be spent in silence.

"Grandpa, I didn't know you were going to tell such a sad story," Honey whimpered, hugging Snickers close to her. "Besides, I thought this story was about me bein' tall."

"Now what makes you think this story is gonna be sad?" Grandpa challenged. "And there really *is* going to be a lesson in it for you. Can you trust me on that?"

"Sure I can, Grandpa," Honey answered more softly, loosening her grip on Snickers. "It's just I can imagine how Becky or Rebecca—what was her name?—must have felt—especially when she was supposed to be taking care of the mama dog and *then* the puppy—when they each got into trouble. I think I'd feel about like *dyin'* if somethin' like that happened to Snickers."

Chapter 8

Attention on Florence

"The little girl's name was Rebecca. But unless she was in trouble, everybody called her 'Becky.' In the past, I couldn't have understood how she felt, but now I can," Grandpa admitted. "Now, how about some more of that story?" he asked.

When Honey half-grinned and nodded, Grandpa continued his tale.

> Arriving at the W, Casey and Billy Bob found a woman who gave them directions to the cave. The cave was once a mine shaft that had fallen-in long before the Warrens bought the place. According to the woman, from the sound of the puppy's whines, the shaft or cave sounded pretty deep.
>
> Near the cave Casey and Billy Bob saw several cowboys, their horses grazing or tied to shrubs. Many kinds and lengths of ropes lay around the area. The two new arrivals dismounted and left their horses to graze near the others.

> To one side a group of three females sat together on a long log. The oldest of the group seemed to be the mother of the other two. She looked upset that she could do nothing to help. In the middle sat the youngest—Becky—who looked like she had been cryin' for some time. On the other side of Becky was the most beautiful creature Casey had ever seen.

Grandpa stopped talking a moment, cleared his throat as if it suddenly was sore, then blew his nose noisily before continuing.

> This beautiful creature was about twenty years old, a few years younger than Casey. She sat with her arm wrapped around her little sister. Although she felt sad for Becky, she chose to look strong for her sister's sake. She stayed by Becky's side, watching the men work, and whispering encouragement.
>
> "Earth to Casey! Earth to Casey! Cowboy, you all right?" Billy Bob joked, noticing Casey's trancelike stare. Casey, snapping to attention, nodded. Billy Bob grinned, "Her name is Florence."
>
> Immediately, Casey really did come alive, startled by the sound of a shotgun blast. "No worries, folks. Rattlesnake over here, but I got him," a proud young cowboy announced, holding a still-wiggling specimen just below the rattlers, and flashing a brilliant smile at Florence.

Instead of being impressed by the show-off, Florence gave him a blistering look, as Becky broke into fresh sobs. Florence held her sister closer and managed to calm the little girl.

"Just what that little kid needed: a reminder of the way this puppy's mama died! That guy's not too smart, is he?" Billy Bob remarked, looking at the now-red-faced braggart.

A warm breeze blew gently from the south. Casey saw Troubles appear, trotting happily from the north. Casey thought to himself, *Perfect timing!*

Billy Bob may not be impressed with my dog. But if Troubles can cheer Becky...and make me look good to Florence, I'll let him have the steak tonight. And I'll gnaw the bone!

"Here, Troubles!" Casey called proudly. A few heads—Florence's among them—turned first to see the source of the words, and then to view the object of Casey's loving tone. A warm, sincere smile crossed Florence's lovely face as she looked at the little dog that ran eagerly to meet his master.

Florence had turned to look again at Casey just as the wind switched directions. Suddenly a look of disgust replaced her beautiful smile. About the time Troubles raced past Florence and her family, Casey and the rest of the cowboys also caught the unmistakable aroma of skunk!

"Casey, get that danged mutt of yours out of here!" about ten people hollered all at once. Embarrassed, especially in front of Florence, Casey removed his hat and waved it at Troubles to shoo him away. To Troubles, Casey's waving the hat was like your mother calling you using your full name. The cowdog knew he was in BIG trouble. As quickly as he had appeared, Troubles disappeared again.

The "skunk" incident got Casey's mind back on track. He had made a poor impression by calling his stinky dog into the crowded area. Defeated in love, Casey gave his full attention to rescuing the puppy for Little Becky.

As Grandpa was ready to shift into high gear with the rescue story, Snickers awoke, rolled off Honey's lap, ran to the door, and began whining. "Uh, oh, Grandpa! I think I'd better let Snickers out for a bit. Out you go, you fuzzy pooch!" Honey laughed. "Come to think of it, I think I could stretch my legs, too. How about you, Grandpa?"

"Indeed, my dear. Sorry about getting so long-winded and makin' you two 'girls' keep sittin'," Grandpa apologized. Standing up stiffly, he got his old cowboy hat from its spot on the "hangin' tree." "Let's go get that ice cream we were talkin' about. I can continue the story about that knock-kneed cowboy on the way. You'd better bring Snickers' leash. With the new health rules, they don't let dogs in the store anymore. But you can hitch her to the old hitchin' post, just like she was a horse from days gone by."

"Being happy doesn't mean that everything is perfect. It means that you've decided to look beyond the imperfections."

—Author unknown

Chapter 9

Wannabe Heroes

On the way to the ice cream parlor, Grandpa began, "Let's see: I was tellin' you a story. Where was I?"

"Casey and Billy Bob were at a cave to rescue Becky's puppy. Then Troubles showed up smellin' like a skunk, and Casey chased him off," Honey reminded him.

"Oh, yeah. Now I remember. I need to back up a little and tell about the rescue, because that's important to the story," Grandpa replied.

> **After Casey came out of his trance about Florence, he saw what had happened so far to rescue Becky's puppy from the cave. The first problem was that the entrance was too narrow for a man to get in. So, several cowboys had connected strong ropes together and fastened the different lines onto the saddle horn of four different horses. When signaled, each cowboy slowly backed his horse. Pulling together, they had removed two boulders from the entry.**
>
> **Next, they had asked for a volunteer to go down into the cave. First, the volunteer would crawl through the still-narrow entry. Then he would signal the guys on horseback to move forward slowly. The same four ropes used to move the huge rocks would be used to lower him into the cave.**

When the volunteer got below, he would find the puppy and prepare to bring it up. When ready, the man would signal someone above. The same four cowboys would back their horses up. And the four strong ropes would raise the volunteer and the puppy to the surface.

"At least, that was the *plan*," said Grandpa, continuing. "It didn't turn out quite the way they had expected."

"Oh, no! You mean Becky didn't get her puppy back? Did... did it *die?*" Honey asked, almost in tears.

"Now that wasn't what I said. What happened is that the roughest, toughest, bowleggedest cowboy wanted to be the hero. So, he got all hitched-up into the ropes and started crawling into the cave," Grandpa smiled.

> At first everyone thought his big belly wasn't going to let him get through, but somehow he made it that far. It looked like he might be able to slide on through the opening, but then his legs stopped him from getting through. The fella squirmed and wiggled, but his bowed legs simply took up more width than the opening would allow.
>
> It took a while to get him out because his belly was wedged between those rocks. Getting that belly out was like trying to pull a marshmallow through the slot in a piggy bank. It was tough enough him gettin' in even halfway, but gravity was workin' against them tryin' to pull him out. By the time they got him out, the horses were covered with sweat, and the not-so-proud-anymore cowboy had some pretty painful skinned places around his middle.

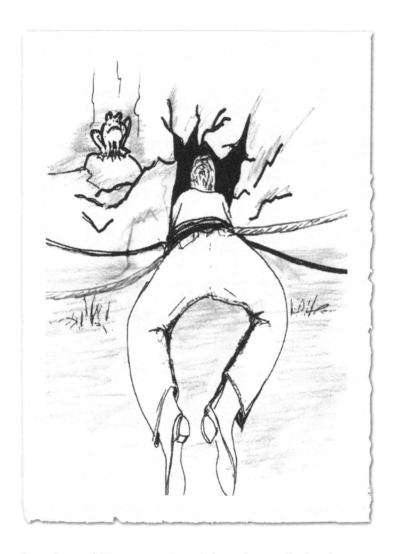

Grandpa and Honey continued their slow walk the short distance into town. From time to time Snickers disappeared into shrubs and underbrush, either to check out the wildlife or to escape the two humans who only wanted to talk. Honey doubted that Grandpa *really* needed to walk that slowly. It seemed that his pace was simply keeping time with his story.

As soon as Grandpa finished the description of the first rescue attempt, he launched into the description of the second.

The second hero-wannabe had seen what a problem it was to remove the first one. However, without a large belly, this next-to-the-roughest, next-to-the-toughest, next-to-the-bowleggedest cowboy volunteered even before the first was freed from the cave's opening.

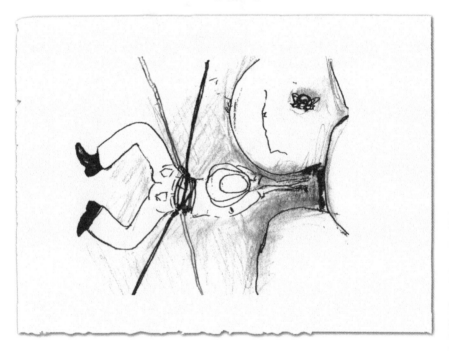

While the ropes were being attached, Wannabe Hero Number Two nodded and winked at Miss Florence. Sure of his success, he flexed his biceps, flashed another toothy grin, and got down on his hands and knees to enter the cave. Then with arms stretched together above his head, he slithered, snakelike, into the opening. He looked as if he might get through. But this cowboy "walks with forked leg."

"Huh? What do you mean, Grandpa?"

"A lot of people distrust snakes. Since a snake's tongue is divided at the tip, if someone '*speaks* with a forked tongue,' his words are like a snake's: He can't be trusted. This second cowboy was like a snake in several ways. But the reason he wasn't getting into the cave was that his legs were wide—split apart like a snake's tongue. He wiggled and slithered, but he was too bowlegged to get through the opening," Grandpa explained with a smirk.

"The horses backed this guy out of the hole with less effort than they had the first guy. Wannabe Number Two was not flexin' his muscles or showing-off anymore. He just put on his hat, ducked his head as he walked past the ladies, and returned to his horse," Grandpa said, this time with a big grin.

"Grandpa, you look happy. The puppy's still down in the cave. How can you be so happy when Becky must be sad?" Honey asked in an *almost*-disrespectful tone.

"Sorry, Honey. You're right: Little Becky was *very* upset. She cried when the big-bellied guy couldn't get her pup, but she *really* howled when the second guy gave up right away. She figured if the roughest, toughest, bowleggedest cowboys in the county couldn't rescue her pup, she might not get it back."

Things were pretty quiet for a while, except for Becky's sobs, that is. All the tough cowhands were confused by the failure of the two best all-around cowboys. The rest of the men didn't want to fail. So, they looked for a way to shift responsibility to anyone else.

Knowing Casey was a popular target for teasing, someone called out: "Hey, how about you, Casey? You're quite a specimen of a cowboy! Let's see you rescue the little girl's pup!" Then, several cowboys called out, "Yeah, Casey! We double-dog dare you!"

Next thing you know, somebody shoved Casey to a spot in the middle of the crowd. There he stood, all eyes on him. Were the cowboys just looking for more proof that Casey wasn't a real cowboy? Or did Casey really stand a chance to get the little girl's puppy out?

"You cannot be lonely if you like the person you're alone with."

—Dr. Wayne W. Dyer

Born 1940
Internationally renowned author and speaker on self-development
Spent his childhood in orphanages and foster homes

Chapter 10

Drama at the Ice Cream Parlor

At that point in the story they reached the ice cream store. As Grandpa had said, a hitching post stood near the front door. Honey whistled for Snickers and snapped her leash on. "There, now, you be a nice horsey, okay?"

Grandpa told Honey, "Snickers will be fine there. Everybody here watches out for each other's pets."

When Honey stepped inside the ice cream "parlor" (as it was called years ago), she felt that she had stepped back in time a half-century. Beside each small table stood two wrought iron seats topped with cushions in old-timey country patterns. Yellowed black-and-white photographs—apparently of Sandy Gulch and her citizens decades ago—dotted the faded walls of the parlor.

The walls looked like they hadn't been painted, nor the pictures dusted, in years. But the kitchen area looked spotless. The creamy-looking hand-dipped ice cream and selection of locally-made candies tempted anyone who entered.

After ordering, Honey wandered about the parlor looking at the old photographs. These photos were taken long before she was born, but some of the people looked familiar. When Grandpa brought their orders to the table, Honey quickly joined him. "How long has this 'parlor' been here, Grandpa?"

"Oh, it's been an ice cream parlor for about 35 years," he answered. Eagerly he dug into the whipped cream on his Honey Pecan Crunch sundae. "Say, how is that bubble gum-and-blueberry sundae with strawberry topping, Girl?"

"Omigosh! It's *heavenly*! Wanna taste it?" Grandpa's face clearly gave his answer. Changing the subject again, she asked, "Say, Grandpa, do you know any of those people in the pictures?"

"I do, or in some cases I *did*," Grandpa answered a bit sadly. "But if I start tellin' stories about all those people, you'll never learn what happened to Becky's puppy *or* Casey's knock-knees. Do you want me to finish Casey's story first?"

Honey's nod encouraged Grandpa to continue.

> So there Casey was, standin' in the middle of a crowd of people who came to get Becky's puppy back for her. The two best cowboys in the bunch had failed. And now the guys who had always razzed him the most about his legs had put him on the spot.
>
> If this was a "set-up" to torment Casey, these cowboys could make sure he failed. And he'd never live it down. On the other hand, maybe he really could get Becky's puppy back for her.
>
> Suddenly, he forgot about what might go wrong and how embarrassed he might become. One look at little Becky told him what was right. With a strong heart, he turned to the cave and walked purposefully to the ropes that had been thrown in the dirt. There was no doubt Casey intended to get the puppy for Becky.
>
> Just then he heard a sudden sound. Looking over his shoulder, he saw the entire Warren family—including Mr. Warren—clapping and cheering for Casey. Nobody had ever cheered for him before. Their encouragement felt strange, but he really liked it. He hoped he could live up to their dreams.

Ropes tied around Casey's middle, horses and riders in place, the knock-kneed cowboy began crawling forward, just as the others had done. Without bowed legs or a big belly, he entered easily through the narrow opening into the cave. Carefully, slowly, step by step, the four riders—each some 30 or more yards from the cave's opening, guided their mounts forward, allowing Casey to descend slowly.

Inside the cave, Casey was surprised how dark it suddenly became. To calm himself and the puppy, he began singing an old cowboy song. He'd sung only a little when he heard the puppy crying. Thinking the pup didn't like his song, Casey switched to talking softly. "Hey, little fella.[6] You're not all alone anymore. I'm comin' down for a visit. Then we'll leave here together. Is that okay with you, little guy?"

Aboveground, it seemed to Becky that she might get her puppy back safe and sound. Becky began cheering, clapping, and dancing about. Happy for her, first a few—then many—of the onlookers began cheering with her.

At the edge of the crowd, unnoticed by anyone, a man stood, his face darkened by shadow and rage.

As Casey continued being lowered into the cave, his eyes began adjusting to the darkness. Some twenty yards below him on a rocky ledge, Becky's puppy sat shivering and whimpering. Although Casey was afraid a loud noise would scare the puppy, he shouted up to those on the surface.

---

6 fella = fellow: a man or boy

An older cowboy near the cave's entrance held his palm up to the crowd to silence the chatter, while leaning closer and cupping the other palm behind his ear. "Quiet, ever'body! He's sayin' something," the cowboy announced. Then after a moment, he added, "That ole knock-kneed cowboy says he can see your puppy, little girl!"

Hearing that Casey had found the puppy, the Warren family began hugging. The crowd cheered.

After a brief time, the older cowboy quieted everyone again. "Hush, now," he said. "We need to hear what Casey's sayin' to us. Men on horseback need to know exactly what to do." Everyone wondered just how deep the old cave really was and how long before Casey and the puppy would come out.

"Too many people overvalue what they are not and undervalue what they are."

—Malcolm S. Forbes
1919–1990
Publisher of Forbes magazine

Chapter 11

Casey's Head Spins

Grandpa took a deep breath and a bite of his ice cream, then continued his story.

While others were celebrating the news that Casey had seen the puppy, the enraged cowboy slipped out of sight to the far side of his horse, quietly removing something from his gear.

At the moment the old cowboy silenced the crowd, a huge "BOOM!!!" was heard a few feet behind two of the cowboys who controlled the ropes. Everyone was startled by the deafening sound so close. The cowboys lost control of their spooked horses, which bolted forward several steps.

Belowground, two of Casey's ropes suddenly loosened, slamming him hard into a wall of the cave. Pain shot through the right side of his body like a bolt of lightning.

Immediately a second "BLAM!!!!" split the air and peppered the other two rope men with shot.

Casey's head was trying to clear from getting slammed against the wall when the remaining two ropes—on which his safety depended—suddenly loosened. Casey plummeted to the ledge where the puppy lay.

Honey, fully taken in by the drama and the fear, put her spoon down and leaned closer to Grandpa to catch every word.

Troubles, sensing that his master was in danger, appeared just as the mystery man had put his shotgun away and was about to make his escape. The man already had his left foot in the stirrup and was in the process of swinging his right foot over his horse's back. Suddenly Troubles lunged and caught the man by the pants leg.

Overtaken by the impact of the mighty midget mutt, the troublemaker was caught with his left foot in the stirrup and no way to free his right leg. Powerless in his position—and overcome by the dense stench of skunk (which clung on Troubles like invisible glue)—the mystery man passed out cold.

Troubles was excited that his courage would now be rewarded. As four or five cowboys rushed to congratulate the brave cowhound, Troubles stood proud, barely slobbering, still gripping the bad guy's pants leg tightly between strong, clenched teeth. Finally, the cowboys would see Troubles as the brave hound he was!

Wha-a-a-t?!!? Did the cowboys praise Troubles for his courage? No! Did they scratch him behind his royal ears? No! Did they award him blue ribbons for his prizeworthy catch? No way! Each cowboy took off his hat—not to bow before the princely Troubles—but to shoo him away!

"Get outta here you stinky mutt!" one yelled.

"We got rid of you awhile ago! Now git-fer-good[7], you cursed cur!" another shouted, swinging his hat at Troubles and creating a miniature tornado that disturbed the hair on the hound's back.

"Get outta here; let us perfeshunuls[8] take over, you sorry mongrel!" another bellowed, his boot grazing Troubles' rear.

Troubles wisely released his death grip on Pretty Boy's pants leg, tucked his tail between his legs, and darted away. Cowering at a safe distance, the helpless hero saw the bad guy regaining consciousness and struggling to resist the cowpunchers' arrest. It didn't take long, though, for the five tough cowboys to hog-tie "Pretty Boy" to get him ready for the sheriff.

"'Pretty Boy.' He was that 'snake' guy that had been showin' off his muscles for Miss Florence, wasn't he?" Honey asked perceptively. "I knew I didn't like him when you told about him tryin' to get into the cave. Hey, I'll bet he's the same guy that had killed the rattlesnake a little earlier. Am I right, Grandpa?"

"You're catchin' on so fast, Honey, that *you* might need to finish tellin' this story!" Grandpa chuckled.

"What I don't understand, Grandpa, is why that snake-guy did that. And why didn't the horses jump around when he shot the snake?"

---

7   Git-fer-good= get-for-good: go away permanently
8   Perfeshunuls = professionals: trained experts in a certain field

"Good questions," Grandpa began. "Let me answer the second question first. Horses on cattle ranches often are used to hearing gunfire, at least at a distance. When 'Pretty Boy' shot the snake, he was away from the crowd a distance. *And* he was using an ordinary shotgun shell, probably loaded with something that would be used for hunting dove or quail.

"When he was up close, though, he wanted to cause some problems. So, he used super-powered ammunition that made a lot of noise and stung those guys' skin like a mess of hornets. It's a wonder he didn't hurt them really bad or cause the old shotgun to blow up in his own face. Turned out, though, that pack of angry cowboys kinda messed-up Pretty Boy's face," Grandpa said, beaming almost ear to ear.

"Now for your first question about why he did it. Have you ever noticed, Honey, that some people just can't stand for anyone else to win?" Honey, diving back into her sundae, nodded silently. "Well, this guy was one of those people. He'd tried twice to show off for Florence, and both times his plan backfired. Now, this knock-kneed guy shows up. He's not *nearly* as good-lookin' nor near the cowboy that Pretty Boy was. And...."

"Okay, let me see if I've got it," Honey interrupted, grinning. "The pretty, snaky guy couldn't stand it that Miss Florence was impressed by someone like Casey! Right?"

"Bingo! You've got it! Okay, Honey, now how about tellin' me the rest of the story?" Grandpa winked, savoring a big spoonful of his own Honey Pecan Crunch ice cream. Honey got quiet to hear what Grandpa said next.

> The people up top didn't know exactly what was happening to Casey. But judging by how far those rope-horses ran, everyone figgered[9] Casey was in pretty bad shape.
>
> When he kept howling in pain, the folks knew he was alive. Then, after a little while everything got quiet below.

Grandpa leaned back in his chair as if finished with the story, and then began eating his melting ice cream.

"Nuh-uh, Grandpa! I'm not gonna let you quit there! Tell me what happened next to Casey. What happened to that puppy?" Honey begged.

"I figured you might be getting' tired of hearing this old man's ramblin' story. So I thought I'd just give your ears a break," Grandpa teased.

Seeing Honey's mock anger, he continued.

> Well, Casey was in a lot of pain... enough, in fact, that he was worried that he might pass out. If that happened, although Casey might be rescued, the puppy wouldn't be.
>
> So, while his brain was still workin' a little, he quit his yellin' and concentrated on calling the puppy to him. Balanced on the dark ledge, Casey unbuttoned his jacket, managed to get the puppy inside it, and rebuttoned it. He took a few deep breaths to relax and checked the ropes to see they would hold. Then he called topside to be lifted.

---

9   Figgered = figured: calculated, decided

It seemed like hours before Casey saw light at eye level. When he reached a flat spot that went sideways instead of straight up, Casey realized he had no use of his legs. He would have to use his arms to lift his body any farther.

One thing he could do was move himself onto a ledge. Doing so gave him the chance to unbutton his jacket and let the puppy loose. It took longer than expected to get the little dog to a place where it could stand.

Once all four feet were on solid ground, the puppy crept out of the cave, stepping carefully and blinking in the brightness. All at once, a huge cheer went up from the crowd. And Becky raced forward to hug her puppy.

"Mollie, I love you!" Becky cried, tears of joy rolling down her swollen face. "Please don't ever scare me like that again!" In answer to her mistress's request, Mollie licked the salty tears from Becky's face.

In the excitement of watching the puppy and child, everyone forgot Casey. *At least the horses haven't run off, and my ropes are holding. But it won't be easy gettin' out of this hole since I can't move my legs,* Casey thought.

Painfully, Casey rolled onto his stomach. Inch by inch, using his arms, he pushed and pulled himself up a slight slope toward the light. He hadn't realized how strong gravity was until he tried to leave the cave without using his legs. As he wondered if he was going to have to do all the work alone, he heard a familiar voice several feet away.

"Hey, Casey, you okay in there?" a worried Billy Bob asked.

"Well, sure," Casey said sarcastically. "Except for hurtin' all over and my legs not movin', I'm just fine. What's goin' on up there?"

"Keep calm, pardner,"[10] Billy Bob replied. "Y'er alive, and that's better than we thought it might've been. How far back in the cave are ya, can ya tell?"

"Mebbe ten feet or so. Problem is, from where I am, it's uphill. All the ropes are still tied around my waist, but it might be kinda nice if I had somethin' down here to help me slide over these sharp rocks. Since I can't use my legs, I'll be slidin' and tearin' all the hide off my belly and legs," Casey explained. "Besides, I'm hurtin' so bad I feel like I'm gonna pass out any time now."

"Uh-oh, this isn't soundin' too good for Casey! Your story's startin' to scare me, Grandpa," Honey said, wide-eyed.

---

10 pardner= partner: a friendly, informal term used for someone of equal status; an ally.

"Let every man be respected as an individual and no man idolized."

—Albert Einstein

1879–1955
German-born, world-famous physicist
Named "Person of the Century" by Time magazine in 1999
The name "Einstein" has become synonymous with genius.
Some sources say Einstein learned to speak later than usual and was dyslexic.

Chapter 12

The Womanly Art of Rescue

"Don'tcha worry, Honey. There's one feisty young woman who's gonna get things figgered out! Matter of fact, she kinda reminds me of another young lady I know," Grandpa grinned.

"Of me?" Honey inquired.

Grandpa only winked before continuing his tale.

> Outside the cave, most of the crowd hushed at once. It was Florence who broke away and joined Billy Bob at the cave's opening. "What's happened to Mr. Casey[11], gentlemen? Where is he?" she asked in a panicked tone.
>
> "Well, ma'am," one of the older cowboys replied, "it sounds like he's in a bit of trouble. Cain't seem t'git his legs t'workin'. D'ya have anythang at the house that he might lay on to slide him over the rocks?"

---

11 Mr. Casey: In the South, especially in the past, addressing adults by their first name—especially someone the speaker did not know well—was considered disrespectful. To be polite, people often said "Mr." or "Miss" (or even "Aunt" or "Uncle" if the person was a close friend of the family) before the first name. "Ma'am" and "Sir" were also used frequently as a sign of respect, usually with someone older, but also with someone of a higher social status to whom respect was expected.

"I'm sure we do.... Oh, I know just the thing," she answered quickly. Then leaning close to the opening, she spoke loudly enough for Casey to hear and feel encouraged, "Mr. Casey, I can't thank you enough for getting my little sister's puppy for her. Right now, though, I want you to know we'll get you out of there in no time! You just hang on and don't get discouraged," she said in a cheerful voice.

She turned to a man who worked for her dad. In a self-confident tone, she requested, "Mr. Jake, would you please run to the tack house? Inside are some old woolen blankets and some thick saddle pads. Bring a stack of each of those and 20 yards or so of lightweight, soft cotton rope. Oh, and a cane pole with a strong line and a hook on it."

Jake returned quickly with the items. Taking the blankets and pads from him, Florence spread several thicknesses of blankets on the hard ground. Next, she placed a few thick saddle pads on top. Then she covered the pads with more blankets, making a sort of "saddle pad sandwich."

She instructed the nearby cowboys to make a long, skinny roll for her. "Please roll this all up as tight as you can, because we've got to slide it through that narrow opening," she explained.

When the men had done this, Florence quickly tied the roll in soft rope in such a way that the cowboys were amazed. They had no idea any woman—especially one so young—could work with rope so quickly and effectively. That roll was going to stay tight until Casey pulled his end of the rope the right way.

"Uh,... Miss Florence, ma'am, what about this fishin' pole ya had me bring?" Jake asked cautiously, feeling foolish about questioning the capable young cowgirl.

"Great question, Mr. Jake," Florence answered. "Let me talk to Mr. Casey for just a minute; then we'll set it all up." Stretching out flat, stomach down, near the opening of the cave, she called to Casey, who was ready to know what was happening aboveground.

"Mr. Casey, can you hear me? Are you doing okay in there?" Hearing his answer, she continued, "I can see down the entryway a fair distance. I'm thinking you're not too far beyond that. What we're going to do is slide one end of a cane fishin' pole to you. With a little luck, you're going to be able to grab the end and pull on it. Once you have it in your hand, I'll explain what happens next. Okay?"

From underground she heard Casey's answer. "Yes, ma'am, I understand. I think I'll probably be able to reach that pole because when you spoke then, I could see a shadow on the ceiling. I'm doin' okay enough that I'll do whatever you say."

Then she turned her attention back to preparing the materials. "Okay, Mr. Jake, I need you to bury that fishhook deep into this end of the roll so Mr. Casey doesn't get it buried in his hand. I don't want to have to commit surgery on him to get it out." After Jake did as she requested, he handed her the big end of the pole.

Scooting as close to the entry as possible, again Florence called out, "Mr. Casey, it's me again. Are you ready to come out of your hiding place now?" she asked jokingly.

The sound of her voice caused Casey's heart to pound, and he forgot the pain in his legs for a few moments. *Surely she can hear this noise inside my chest,* he thought. But he answered calmly, "I'm ready, Miss Florence. Just tell me what I need to do."

"I'm pushing the pole toward you right now," she explained. "As soon as you can see it, you'll need to tell me whether to angle it closer to your right side or your left. Here goes."

For several seconds, Florence threaded the pole into the cave; and Casey kept watching for it to appear. When she'd pushed it nearly as far as she could from where she was lying, she asked, "Mr. Casey, can you see the pole yet?"

"I think I'm seeing a bit of its shadow over on my right side. Problem is, the cave falls off steeply there and we'll probably lose it. Can you move it farther to my left side, and slide it down about six more feet?" he asked, trying to keep the intense pain out of his voice.

Not telling him how that would have to happen, Florence answered in a cheerful, confident voice, "Anything for our chief puppy-rescuer!" Then, without warning the others, she shifted the pole over to her right and began sliding into the entrance.

"Miss Florence, what in tarnation[12] are you doin'?!!" Jake exclaimed. "Mr. Amos will kill me if I let you go in there. Now, come on out, girl. Let some of us men do that!"

"You so-called men should've already done it!" she retorted. "Now, make yourself useful by loopin' a rope over my ankles in case you need to drag me out. And quit pestering me with your worries! I've got work to do!"

---

[12] tarnation: a term use in New England and Southern U.S. to express anger or annoyance.

"Self pity is our worst enemy and if we yield to it, we can never do anything wise in the world."

—Helen Keller

1890–1968
Became deaf and blind at the age of 19 months
Anne Sullivan taught her to communicate with sign, spoken, and written language. Keller learned Braille, and read in English, French, German, Greek, and Latin.
She wrote 2 books, and acted in a movie.

Chapter 13

Casey's Visitors

"Wow! She *is* a sassy woman, isn't she?" Honey laughed. Grandpa could tell by the admiration in her voice that Honey would become that sort of woman someday. It gave his heart a thrill to hear his granddaughter speak admiringly of Florence.

"Ah, Honey, you don't know the half of it. You just don't know the half of it," Grandpa smiled, with a faraway look in his sparkling blue eyes.

> Casey couldn't hear what the folks outside were saying, but he gathered from Florence's words that he was about to have a bit of company in the cave. *Who'd've thought we'd meet again like this?* Casey thought to himself, smiling in spite of his pain.
>
> All thoughts of pain soon vanished when Casey saw the flicker of shadows on the ceiling of the cave. On his left side, above his head, appeared the end of the cane pole. "I can see the end of the pole now, Miss Florence. But it's way over my head. There's no way for me to reach it."

"No problems, Cowboy," Florence answered confidently, in a voice that inspired Casey. "You'll reach it in just a few seconds. When you get it, just keep pulling it down to you." Scooting forward as far as she could, she shoved the pole ahead a few more feet—just enough that the heavy end see-sawed down, inches from Casey's reach. Then, stretching even more, she sent the pole sliding down the incline until Casey answered.

"Got it!" Casey shouted happily.

There in the semi-darkness, the two discussed how they would get Casey from the cave. Directed by Florence, Casey pulled the pole and then the blanket roll. He used his pocket knife to cut the hook free. Then he pulled the roll to a clear space, untied the rope, and unrolled the blankets.

Casey moved painfully onto the homemade "mattress," which would protect him from the sharp edges of the cave's floor. Next, Florence told him how to protect his legs with the "mattress" and rope. "That rope has to hold those blankets in place while the horses are pulling you over this rocky floor," she explained.

Directed by Florence, Casey tied the blankets securely around his legs. Next Florence reminded him that the ropes which had lifted him to this point would now be used to slide him out of the cave's opening.

When Casey was ready, Florence, careful not to get caught in the ropes, shouted instructions for the mounted cowboys. "Back the horses s-l-o-w-l-y and smoothly." Meantime, Casey held onto the ropes and used his arms to take some weight off the rocks under his bruised body. Sometimes he rolled slightly side to side to miss the roughest edges. After a couple minutes, he had to rest. The strength was leaving his body.

"It's okay. We're in no hurry. The dance doesn't begin for a couple more hours," Florence teased, well aware that it would be a while before Casey would dance again.

Her little joke was the encouragement Casey needed to keep going. He remembered his grandmother's saying that *A merry heart does good like a medicine.* "If you can keep me laughing, those guys may be able to drag me out of here after all," Casey chuckled.

For the next few minutes, Florence acted silly and told goofy jokes to Casey. Silly or not, the light-hearted chatter kept Casey's mind off the pain from the rocks under his bruised body.

About the time she had him laughing, Florence also heard a whine close by. "AAaaahhh! Skunk!" she yelled, forgetting how loud her voice could sound in a closed-in rocky space. "Casey, your dog is in here, too! Go away! Shoo! Get out of here,"

"Troubles, get outta here!!" Casey yelled in his meanest voice. "How do you always manage to show up at the absolute worst time?"

Whimpering as if he'd been kicked, Troubles turned around and scooted back out the passage. When he was gone and they could breathe freely again, Casey joked, "That danged mutt sure knows how to ruin a romantic moment!" The people outside must have wondered how the two inside the cave could be laughing at such a serious time.

Once Casey was within arm's length, Florence's chatter grew quieter and even more optimistic. She could see from the look in Casey's eyes that he was suffering more than he admitted. Keeping constant eye contact, she backed out of the cave at the same rate that he was sliding forward.

As Florence's feet and backside reappeared, concerned cowboys, ranch hands, and her dad readied a stretcher and pillow made from the extra blankets and pads. The tailgate on a neighbor's pickup was lowered and its bed piled deep with soft hay to cushion Casey's ride to the hospital.

After Florence slid out of the cave, she stood up, looked her father in the eye, and shook her head side-to-side slightly. Her look said, *He's not looking so great.* She stepped away from the entrance. Strong men moved forward for the really tough part: guiding Casey's upper body through the narrow opening.

Chapter 14

Mr. Warren Steps Up

"Florence knew what she was doin', didn't she? She sure sounded braver and smarter than those cowboys," Honey smiled.

"She was an amazing woman, Honey," Grandpa answered seriously. "She made it possible to get Casey that far. Now it was time for her to hand the reins over to her dad."

Mr. Warren was happy to step up to help. "Casey, it's me: Amos Warren," he began, speaking slowly and carefully. He was unsure how alert Casey was. "We think you may have taken quite a tough fall down there. So we want to make it as easy on you as possible getting the rest of the way out. Can you understand me okay?"

"Huh?…Yeah, a little bit," Casey struggled with the understanding and the reply.

"Casey, try to stay awake just a bit longer. We think you have injured your legs pretty badly. Would you check the rope holding them? It needs to be tied so it will hold your legs together and won't slip off when we slide you out the opening. If your legs are broken, that rope can keep more damage from happening. Can you do that for me?" Mr. Warren waited for Casey's answer.

Casey didn't reply immediately, not a good sign. But when he did speak, it was to say he had done what Mr. Warren asked. "Okay, sir. That rope should hold the blankets in place. Now what?"

"Try to hold on to the ropes and the top of those blankets as you're sliding out," Mr. Warren spoke slowly so that Casey would understand. "And if you need us to stop so you can fix the ropes again, give a shout."

At Mr. Warren's signal, the horsemen on the ropes each backed their mounts up one step. Other signals from Mr. Warren followed, each accompanied by a corresponding tug on the rope. After several steps backwards, Casey spoke, "Mr. Warren, I'm gettin' real light-headed. The pain is getting' pretty bad, and I feel like I'm gonna pass out. Is it okay if I rest now?"

"Yes, Casey. You've earned a break. You just relax now. These men will have you out before you know it," Mr. Warren answered.

The next few minutes passed like those before, slowly sliding Casey from the cave. On instructions from Mr. Warren, one of the slender but strong young ranch hands approached the cave entrance. He reached in under the now-unconscious Casey's head and shoulders, and guided him into the open air. To the ranch hand, the process was like helping a heifer give birth to her first calf.

Casey, having been "birthed" from the cave, lay still, but breathing, rolled in his blankets and pads. Mr. Warren again took the lead. "Men, we need to pick him straight up, all at the same time and lower him—again, all at the same time—to these blankets and pads we have set out here on the ground. Easy does it."

When this was done, Mr. Warren continued, "Great job, men! Next, we're going to use the blankets to lift him off the ground and onto the hay in the pickup bed. We'll need three or four people on each side and one each at his head and feet."

Once again the men transported Casey carefully and positioned him as comfortably as possible on the straw. Then they closed the tailgate to take Casey to the hospital. By this time, everyone could see that Casey's legs were messed-up pretty bad.

"Grandpa, didn't they have ambulances back then?" Honey asked. "It sounds like taking him in an ambulance would've been a lot better."

"You're right, Honey. It would have been better to have a real ambulance. But they were on the far side of a big ranch, with rough roads. An ambulance might not get there. So, they did the best they could with what they had.

"There's more to this story, but I think it's a good idea to check on Snickers first. Does she need some water?" Grandpa asked.

"I'll check on her, *and* I'll see if the ladies at the counter will give her a little taste of vanilla ice cream." Grandpa raised an eyebrow when Honey mentioned feeding ice cream to Snickers. Quickly Honey added, "I don't let her have it often. Just *once* in a while. Besides, Snicker's 'vet'—Dr. Christina—says vanilla is safe." Honey wasn't sure if Grandpa was really worried about Snickers, or if he liked to be the only one to spoil the pooch.

While Honey was outside caring for Snickers, Grandpa got up to stretch his legs and look at the old photographs that hung on the wall. He paused at a photo of a couple standing outside the ice cream parlor. The man appeared to be in his thirties, the woman several years younger. She held a young child by the hand. There, tied to the hitching post where Snickers now was, stood a horse. On the ground a tiny dog sat, looking up at the child. As he heard Honey approaching, Grandpa returned to their table.

Misty-eyed and blinking, Grandpa asked, "Where were we? Oh, wait! I remember," he said.

Chapter 15

Hospital Visitors

"Grandpa, this day really is turning out different from what Casey expected that morning. He thought he was going to get brand-new legs, didn't he?" Honey asked.

"Good rememberin', Honey. And interesting you thought about the 'new legs' just now," Grandpa replied.

> After they took Casey to the hospital in the bed of the neighbor's pick-up, only the hospital staff saw him for some time. Casey, who was in and out of consciousness, didn't really know what was happening for the next few hours.
>
> That night, though, after he'd had first aid for his injuries and medication for his pain, Casey heard a knock on the door. Into the room walked a heavy, goggle-eyed man dressed in a white lab coat.
>
> "Hello, young man. I'm Dr. Gustafson, but you may call me Dr. Gus," the man announced. His body resembled that of a large toad. He had eyes and a voice that resembled a frog's. "As perhaps you know, your accident messed up both your legs quite badly."

Not waiting for a reply from Casey, Dr. Gus continued in a croaking voice, "You're in luck, though. I am the best orthopedic surgeon in fourteen States, including this one." Looking at Casey's medical chart, Dr. Gus observed, "So, you're a cowboy by occupation. You'll be happy to know that I can fix your legs good-as-new. They'll wrap around a fat cow-pony just like before," he bragged.

"What do you mean?" Casey asked, suspicious that Dr. Gus might not be as great a doctor as stated. "My legs have never wrapped around a cow-pony, fat or otherwise."

"What they were like before makes no difference. I can fix them whichever way you prefer," Dr. Gus replied confidently. "You decide and let me know before your surgery in the morning. Just remember, though, be careful what you wish for. Well, it's time for me to hop on out of here. See you tomorrow."

"Wait a minute, Grandpa. The name *Gus* sounds really familiar. Hey, wasn't that the name of the frog that warned Casey to be careful what he wished for because it might come true?" Honey asked. "And now this froggy-doctor is called Dr. Gus-something?"

"Ah, what wonderful memories young people have!" Grandpa replied, smiling. "You sound surprised, Honey. Don't you think that a frog that is smart enough to talk is also smart enough to know that Casey was making an unwise wish?"

"Uh... well, I guess so," she said, embarrassed to admit that a frog might talk *or* have intelligent thoughts. "But here's

Casey's chance to get something he's always wanted. So, wouldn't he be dumb to change his mind now?"

"Excellent question. But instead of answering it, how about we leave it until later? Then *you* decide after I tell you what happened next," Grandpa suggested.

After Dr. Gustafson left, little Becky—whose puppy had been rescued—walked into the room, accompanied by her dad. It took a moment for Casey to remember who Becky was. The wide grin on her face, though, was a big hint.

"Mr. Casey, I had to beg Daddy to let me come here because he said you wouldn't feel like seeing me." Becky dropped her eyes shyly, then continued. "But I told him I just had to come see you tonight. You did something for me today that nobody but you could've done. You got Mollie back for me. All those braggy cowboys tried, but they couldn't do it.

"I had to thank you, Mr. Casey. You saved my puppy, and I'll always love you for that." Then she handed him a picture. "Mollie and me drew this for you. And Troubles kinda helped, too. That's what Mollie drew right there," Becky said, pointing to something that looked like a puppy paw dipped in red paint.

"And this is me. And that is you. And in the pink dress is my big sister. She likes you. A *lot*," Becky added, quickly looking sideways at her dad, knowing she was going to be in trouble for telling a secret.

"And tell me about these dark orange parts," Casey requested, careful to ignore Becky's secret.

"Oh, that's Troubles' part. After you left we went back to the house. Florence saw Troubles outside and knew he was hungry. So, she brought him some food and called him onto the porch. After he ate, she started givin' him a bath in tomato juice so he didn't keep smellin' like skunk.[13]

"Before she got him rinsed off," Becky continued, "Troubles got away and came to where Mollie and me was makin' your picture. Then Troubles started shakin', and tomato juice went ever'where. Mollie and me didn't have time to make you a clean picture. 'Cause after Troubles splattered us, we had to go take a bath, too."

Casey tried to look sympathetic to Becky about the Troubles story. But even with his legs hurting like crazy, it was all he could do to keep from laughing out loud at her story.

"It's time to get you out of here, young lady, and let Mr. Casey get some rest," said Amos Warren, almost sternly. Then turning to Casey, he added, "Casey, Becky's not the only one who appreciates you. You were very brave today, and you made one little girl very happy.

"I want you to know that you have nothing to worry about. The *Rockin' W* is taking care of the hospital bills. Becky is taking care of Troubles, and Florence is making certain that Horace is cared for. We know you're not going to be ready to go back to your own place when you get out of here. We'll have you a room ready at our house," Mr. Warren smiled.

"That's very generous of you, Mr. Warren. But I don't know when I'd be able to pay you back,"

---

13 A tomato juice bath is a favorite folk remedy for a pet whose fur has been sprayed by a skunk.

Casey replied, worried. "Besides, I can't impose on your hospitality by staying at your house. I thank you very much, though."

"Who said anything about paying me back? If you hadn't been helping Becky, none of this would have happened. This is the least we can do. Besides, you don't have a choice. I'll be here to pick you up from the hospital when you're ready to leave. Now, you rest up, Casey. We'll see you after you wake up from your operation."

Chapter 16

Casey's Big Decision

Strange thoughts and dreams visited Casey all night. Drifting off to sleep, he remembered Becky's saying she loved him. He remembered her telling that Florence liked him. Or was it Florence who loved him and had said that Becky's puppy liked him? When he slept, Casey dreamed his huge, bowed legs got him stuck inside the cave, with no way to get out.

In his dream, when he looked inside the cave, he found hundreds of frogs. Some had stethoscopes draped around their fat necks; some wore surgical masks and gloves. Others were holding huge syringes or scalpels in their froggy hands. The one thing they had in common is that they repeatedly croaked, "Be careful what you wish for. You just might get it!"

"Mr. Casey, Mr. Casey! Wake up!! Are you all right?" a worried nurse asked him.

"Whaaat? Where am I?" Casey asked.

"You're at the hospital because you had a bad accident and broke both your legs. I came in because you were yelling something about being careful what you wish for. Is there something you need?" the nurse asked.

"No. No, I guess not. Thank you. I guess I was just having a bad dream," Casey replied.

In a few minutes, the troubled dreams began again. This time he was being wheeled into the operating room where a huge frog dressed as a surgeon told him, "Well, Mr. Casey. It's time for you to get just what you asked for."

Then the operating room melted away, and he saw Becky—or was it Florence?—crying, "Oh, no! What happened to your legs? I loved you just the way you were!" Next, Troubles began barking at him. Horace laid his ears flat. It was clear that neither dog nor horse liked his bowed legs either. As Casey was trying to explain to his animal friends that he was still Casey - but now with real cowboys' legs—they vanished.

Instead, he found himself surrounded by all the cowboys that were supposed to go on the roundup. In his dream, Casey walked into the Chuckwagon Cafe, so proud of his new handsomely-bowed legs. He was shocked when all the cowboys started laughing and pointing at his legs, nearly doubling-over with laughter.

"What's so dadgummed funny?" the dreaming Casey demanded of the other cowboys. Without a word, they all stood up from the tables where they had been drinking coffee. To Casey's astonishment, every one of them had knocked knees, just like the ones he used to have. "What happened to you guys?" Casey asked.

"I know you won't believe this," said the first, "but I met this frog that talked. I mean, he *really* talked. And he told me I could have knock-knees if I'd like."

"That's what he told me," said another. "Me, too," said a third and a fourth cowboy. "We saw how Miss Florence looked at you," still another said.

The knock-kneed cowboys in the dream faded away, and a different nurse was waking him: "Mr. Casey, it's nearly time for your operation. Dr. Gus is here to speak to you." Sleepily, Casey propped himself up on his elbows as the doctor walked into the room.

"Good morning, young man," Dr. Gustafson croaked. "How about it? Are you ready for a brand-new pair of legs? I can give you whatever kind of legs you wish for. Do you want them to be just a little bit bow-legged, or very bow-legged?" he asked confidently.

In a split-second, Casey was wide-awake and knew what he really wanted. He wanted to be just the way he always was, the sort of person people liked because of who he was on the inside. He knew that if he had to change his looks for someone to admire him, then that person's admiration wasn't worth much. In that moment, he knew he didn't have to look a certain way to accept himself or to have the kind of friends he wanted in his life.

"Thank you, Dr. Gus. But I want to look like me again. Can you fix my knock knees back just the way they were before?" Casey asked. "Knock knees may not suit anybody else, but they're just right for me!"

"If that's what you want, that's what you'll get," Dr. Gus croaked, scratching his warty head in amazement. Then he turned and left the room. Maybe it was the pain medication, but Casey thought he heard a quiet *"Ribbit!"* as Dr. Gustafson hopped away.

As Casey waited for his surgery, his decision puzzled even himself. He still didn't understand quite why he had chosen to keep his knock knees. Maybe it was because those knock knees were the reason little Becky had her puppy again. Maybe it was because he realized imitating someone else didn't lead to happiness. And just maybe he was starting to like himself for the right reasons. Whatever had caused him to change his mind, he felt peaceful about his choice.

Chapter 17

Honey's Lesson

"Wow! That was a neat story, Grandpa! I can see why Casey might be okay staying knock-kneed," Honey replied. Suddenly remembering why Grandpa had told the story, with sad voice she added, "But I still don't see why you think it's good for me to be tall."

"Honey, it's not good *or* bad to be tall *or* short," Grandpa began. "With Casey, even though he couldn't yet put it into words, he had found out that we all have something that we wish were different. If we could just change that *one* thing, we're sure we'd be more attractive; that more wonderful things would happen in our lives—like we *think* happen in others' lives. What we don't know is that even the people we envy have things they'd like to change about *their* own lives."

"I won't argue about that, Grandpa. But all the boys think I'm weird. They don't like tall girls because all the boys want to be taller than the girls they like," Honey countered.

"That may be true about a lot of guys, but I know it's not true about everybody. Besides, think back to Casey just a moment: He had a chance to get his wish. Why do you think he changed his mind?" Grandpa asked.

"Hmmm," Honey smiled. "I guess he changed his mind because he saw that having knocked knees had been a big help. He couldn't have gotten Becky's puppy for her if he'd had bowed legs like he thought he wanted."

"Do you think Casey knew in advance that havin' knocked knees could be an advantage?" Grandpa continued.

Honey closed her eyes and twisted her mouth to one side, as she often did when she was thinking hard. "Well, maybe he could have, if he'd really *tried* to. But I doubt he was trying to think of any," she answered.

"Exactly my point. Now, another question: Can you think of reasons a girl might *want* to be tall?" Grandpa continued.

Eyes closed, mouth twisted, she finally replied, "Like playing basketball maybe? Grandpa, my brain's gonna get tired with all this thinkin'," Honey sighed, pretending to tire of Grandpa's questions. "No, I guess basketball's the only reason I can think of that a girl might want to be tall."

"That's one," Grandpa admitted. "But even if you can't *think* of any more reasons, does that mean there AREN'T any more?"

"No, I guess there could be reasons I wouldn't be able to think of," Honey admitted. "If Casey had spent a year trying to think of good reasons to have knock-knees, I don't think he would have thought they would help him fish a puppy out of a cave." By the way Honey answered, Grandpa could tell that her mind really *was* getting a good work-out.

"Honey, I'm proud of you listening with your heart. What I've found in life is that we can't see beforehand how the very thing we'd like to change is often there for a special reason. The thing we wish we could change may prove important one day. What Casey's story is really all about,

Honey, is that we can be so much happier after we learn to like ourselves however we look."

"Well, I guess so," Honey answered, without sounding totally convinced. "But didn't Casey wish later that he'd decided to get bow legs, like the other cowboys had?"

"You've asked a great question," Grandpa smiled. "Casey still admired bowed legs, it's true. But he'd always remember that his knock knees were just what was needed on that occasion. From that day forward, he began to like himself exactly the way he was. If he had always had the most beautifully-bowed legs in the wild Wild West, some wonderful things would never have happened in his life. If it weren't for his knock knees, you wouldn't be here. Nor would you have Snickers."

"Grandpa, are you kidding me again?" Honey asked suspiciously. "What in the world could Casey's knocked knees have to do with Snickers and me?"

"Someone's opinion of you does not have to become your reality."

—Les Brown

Born 1945
Motivational speaker; author
In 5th grade he was labeled "educably mentally retarded."
Today he would likely be labeled as having ADHD.
"They said I was slow; so I held to that pace," he says in his book
Live Your Dreams.

Chapter 18

The Family Trees

"I see I'm going to have to tell you a bit more of Casey's story," Grandpa smiled. With a far-away look in his eyes, he began.

> Mr. Warren made good on all the promises he made to Casey in the hospital. When the still-knock-kneed cowboy left the hospital and could walk with crutches, a comfortable bedroom was ready for him.
>
> Even Troubles had a little house outside Casey's room. Although the skunk-loving pooch no longer came inside, he was close enough to protect his master. Soon Becky's dog Mollie—the one Casey had rescued from the cave—was sharing Troubles' new home.
>
> The Warren family also made sure that Casey knew he had a place in the family members' lives. It took Casey several weeks to feel comfortable sitting at every family meal, but everyone made it clear that they loved having him there with them. Especially Florence.
>
> Over the next several months, Casey and Florence became more and more fond of each other. Strangely, they were the last two to see that they belonged together. After Casey had

healed enough that he was working again, he began saving money to buy Florence a ring. When he asked her to marry him, she said yes.

When Casey and Florence married, Mr. and Mrs. Warren gave them a little house of their own near the edge of town. That's the cabin I live in now. Becky gave them one of Troubles and Mollie's puppies. Florence named the puppy Buttons.

Seeing that Honey was finding it hard to keep up with the story, Grandpa paused and asked, "Did you catch all that?"

"You said that for a wedding present Mr. and Mrs. Warren gave Casey and Florence a house, and Becky gave them Buttons, one of Troubles and Mollie's puppies. Right?"

"Right! Now, there's just a little more to this story," Grandpa said.

"A couple of years later, Casey and Florence's first child - a daughter they named Susan—was born. Buttons became Susan's dog and lived until Susan was a teenager.

"And your little dog Snickers is Buttons' great-great-great-grandpup!"

"Wait a minute, Grandpa. I'm gettin' *all* confused," Honey started. Then she paused a few moments, still hunting a missing piece to the puzzle. "You say you live in the house where Casey and Florence made their first home? And Snickers came from Troubles and Becky's little dog? Who *are* all these people you're telling me about?" Honey cried.

Patiently Grandpa replied, "They say a picture's worth a thousand words. This one may be worth even more." He rose from his chair and led Honey to the photograph he'd been staring at when his granddaughter was checking on Snickers. "Honey, I'd like for you to look at this picture carefully for a while and tell me what you see in it."

While Honey stood looking at the photo, Grandpa wondered if he were pushing her too far and too fast. But it was hard for him to see her unhappy with herself: He was determined that she have good reasons to think and feel differently.

"Okay, Grandpa, here's what I see," Honey began. "I see some people and a little dog in front of a building that looks a lot like this one. It even has a hitchin' post, too. Oh, yeah, and a beautiful horse."

"So far, so good," Grandpa admitted. "That building *is* this ice cream parlor. Now, tell me what you can figure out about the people just by looking at them," he continued, confident of his granddaughter's observation skills.

Moving nearer the photo as if trying to focus on details, Honey gasped slightly, surprised. "Oh! That's Casey, and that's Florence, and that's Susan, and... and Buttons," she clapped, pleased with herself. "And is that horse Horace?"

"Right again," said Grandpa. "How did you figure all that out?"

"Well, when I looked closely at the picture, I could see a little bit of Casey's legs showing. And I could tell that they were knock-kneed legs. So, if that was Casey, it made sense that the lady was his wife. Then that was their little girl and the dog Becky had given them for a wedding present," Honey replied logically.

"What else did you notice about Casey and Florence?" Grandpa prodded again.

"Well, at first I thought Casey was a taller man because his head is just a little higher up than Florence's. But then, when you kept asking me to notice things, I saw that he was standing on the porch several inches above street level, where Florence is standing. What I'm seeing, then, is that Casey was shorter than Florence. So, I don't get it, Grandpa. What's all this supposed to mean to me?" she asked, still feeling she was missing something.

"One more question for you; then I'll give you some answers," Grandpa promised. "Why do you suppose that Casey's standing on that porch instead of on the ground beside his wife and daughter?"

"Hmmm ... I guess because he didn't like it that his wife was taller than he was. He wished she was shorter so he would look taller?" Honey guessed.

"Your answer makes sense, but that *wasn't* Casey's reason. You see, it had taken Casey a long time to let himself love Florence. He believed this tall, elegant, beautiful woman wouldn't care for someone who looked like him. After all, he was short. And he didn't look a bit like *he* thought a cowboy 'should' look.

"Before they met, Florence had planned to move to New York for a modeling career. With that kind of beauty and style, he was *sure* she wouldn't love him. Even after he knew she loved him, in pictures he always tried to look tall; but it was for *her*, not for himself," Grandpa concluded.

Honey looked at her grandfather as he wiped a tear from his eye, blew his nose, and pretended to feel no emotions. Odd: until today she'd never realized she was as tall as he was. In a flash of understanding she said, "Hey, wait a minute! What's your *real* name, Grandpa?"

"My real name? Well 'Grandpa,' of course," he kidded.

"No, Grandpa. Your *real* real name," Honey said, trying to be serious.

"Funny you should ask," Grandpa smiled through the last of his tears. "My birth certificate reads 'Kenneth Charles.' Kinfolks called me 'K.C.' for short. Later, people started thinking my family was saying 'Casey'; so 'Casey' just kind of stuck with me after that."

"You were *Casey*?!!" Honey kept silent a few moments. "Then that means my mother 'Suze' was Susan in the story? And Mom's Aunt Beck was Becky?" Honey asked, to be sure she had understood. Then she shook her head, feeling silly at having taken so long to figure out the answers.

"Yep," Grandpa replied. "And this ice cream parlor was our first business as a married couple. I milked the cows every morning and evening, and brought the fresh milk in for your Grandma Flo to turn into ice cream. We ordered different flavors and spices from a catalog. And to sweeten the ice cream, we used honey from the bees on the ranch. In fact, our little store was most famous for our Honey Pecan Crunch ice cream.

"By the time you were born," he continued, "Grandma Flo had become quite ill. Everyone was happy that she lived long enough to hold you and see you learn to sit up by yourself. The first time she saw you, she cooed, 'What a honey!' And, so, that's how you got your name."

Honey turned to look again carefully at the photo. Then she pulled her shoulders back, straightened her spine, raised her chin, and smiled. "I remember some of the older people used to tell me that I looked like Grandma Flo. But I just figured it was because of the color of our hair or something.

You know, except for those old-fashioned clothes she wore, I'd be proud to look exactly like her!" Honey said, squeezing her grandfather's hand.

"Speakin' of lookin' exactly like your Grandma Flo, if she'd been short, she couldn't have gotten Casey—that is, *me*—out of the cave," Grandpa added.

"*Wha-a-a-t?* How's that?" Honey asked.

"You remember she went into the cave as far as she could. Then Casey told her he still couldn't reach the fishin' pole. After that she stretched as far as she could to push it to him. Even by stretching, she could get the pole barely far enough that it would 'see-saw' down to him," Grandpa explained.

"Wow! No wonder Casey—er, ... *you*... were glad she was tall!" Honey remarked.

"So, what d'ya think?" Grandpa asked. "Should I cancel your appointment?"

"What appointment, Grandpa?" Honey asked, feeling that she must have missed another important fact.

"Why, the one with the witch doctor that was going to shrink you down to the small, compact size," Grandpa teased.

Laughing aloud, Honey threw her arms around Grandpa's neck, "No way, Grandpa! I like me just like I am! No tellin' what kind of great things are gonna happen because I'm tall!"

With their ice cream and the story finished, Honey and Grandpa smiled in silent understanding and turned to leave the old ice cream parlor. As they passed the ice cream counter, both saw their reflections in the mirror behind it.

It was then that they each noticed Honey was indeed taller than Grandpa. At that moment, instead of slumping a bit (as she would have earlier that day), Honey looked straight into the mirror, squared her shoulders, lifted her chin, and greeted her own image with an appreciative smile.

Then, looking down slightly into her Grandpa's twinkling eyes, she smiled, "Grandpa, I think we're both okay—exactly the way we are!"

"When you're a beautiful person on the inside, there is nothing in the world that can change that about you. Jealousy is the result of one's lack of self-confidence, self-worth, and self-acceptance. The Lesson: If you can't accept yourself, then certainly no one else will."

—Sasha Azevedo

Model, actress, athlete
Sasha battled epilepsy for nearly 20 years.

Creative Corral

For Adults Who Influence Youngsters

Whether you are a kid who is creative and likes to think about the stories you've read, or an adult who influences youngsters (and believes self-acceptance and acceptance of others are crucial), this section is for you.

Besides a summary ("About the Book"), this section contains tools for creative individuals of all ages to stimulate creative thinking, problem-solving, and empathy.

With such objectives in mind, topics under the headings called "For Discussion" and "Thoughtful Writing" can easily be adapted for various purposes. (Discussion topics can be used for writing experiences; "Thoughtful Writing" can be used to stimulate thought-provoking discussions). May you and the child(ren) you care about create to your hearts' content through the experiences provided for you here.

About the Book:

One Saturday Honey, a fifth-grader, takes her dog Snickers to visit Grandpa, the one human being with whom Honey relates best. Observing that she is slouching and looking sad, Grandpa learns that Honey is upset because the boy she likes has embarrassed her about her height. He launches into a story about a knock-kneed cowboy called Casey, who wishes for bowed legs so he can be like the other cowboys. Through the tale, Honey learns that sometimes the very things we most want to change about ourselves turn out to be the biggest blessings of all.

> "The man who trims himself to suit everybody will soon whittle himself away."

—Charles Schwab

Born 1937
Founder and CEO of the Charles Schwab Corporation
2007–Listed by Forbes 400 list as the 57th richest person in the United States (with a fortune of approximately $5.5 billion). Had trouble with English in school because of his dyslexia.

Campfire Chats:

When cowboys were on cattle drives, they were busy all day rounding-up the strayed cattle and branding or treating the animals for injuries or illnesses. Having penned-up the stock, at night the men would sit around the campfire to share a meal and to swap ideas and stories. Often there would be one cowboy who loved to stir the others up and make them think. They might disagree, but they would enjoy listening to what the others had to say. Here is your opportunity to enjoy similar campfire chats.

1. What was Grandpa's reason for telling the long tale of the knock-kneed cowboy to Honey?

2. What caused Casey to change his mind about getting "new legs"?

3. If you had been in Casey's place, would you make the same choice he did, or would you make a different decision? Explain.

4. If Gus, the fairy godfrog, visited you, what would you request? Explain.

5. What situation in your life is similar either to Casey's or Honey's? (What have you wished you could change about your life?) In what way have you—or *can* you—look at your situation differently?

6. Think of a friend who is unhappy about something in his or her life—something he or she wishes were different. What can you say to help your friend look at the circumstance in a different way?

7. Tell about a time someone received his or her wish but later wished he (or she) *had not* had this wish fulfilled. (The person could even be you.)

8. Which of the quotations scattered throughout the book are most meaningful to you? How could you apply those ideas to your own life, or help a friend with them?

9. In a television program or in a movie, how do you know when something scary is coming? In stories and books, writers use words to create a feeling called "foreboding." When (and what words) did the author use foreboding in this story? How could she have created more foreboding in the cave scene?

Wrangler Logic:

To "wrangle" is to argue or dispute. "Wranglers" (cowboys generally in charge of saddle horses) often had to prove their point with horses, but they were also glad to argue their ideas with other cowboys. Modern-day wranglers use writing as their means of proving their points. Below are some opportunities for you to think creatively and prove your point.

1. The writer of *The Knock-Kneed Cowboy* told part of the story from the dog Troubles' point of view. Choose an animal whose viewpoint you would enjoy. This animal would be a pet of yours or even an unpopular animal (such as a spider, a skunk, or an ant at a picnic). Tell about something that happens as if you *were* this animal.

2. Instead of a frog, what animal would you like to see be able to perform magic or grant special wishes? Write a short tale in which your special animal offers to do something amazing for someone.

3. Choose one of the following subjects (or make up one of your own). Write about a way to look at the subject differently:

    a. A friend's grandmother has been really ill and is not expected to live very long. Your friend is very sad.

    b. The teacher accused your best friend of cheating on a test. Now your friend is so angry that he/she will not listen to the teacher or do any homework.

    c. A good friend's parents have decided to divorce. Your friend is upset with both parents.

d. A cousin of yours is really smart in many ways. Because of the cousin's poor performance in school, though, she (or he) will repeat the grade next year.

e. A friend is very creative and has a challenge paying attention to the teacher. Today your friend was embarrassed again when he/she didn't hear the teacher call his/her name.

f. Your friend is the oldest child in the family. Her parents make her do more than what she thinks is her "fair share" of the chores around the house. How can she look at this "unfairness" differently?

g. A friend or cousin is the youngest of the children in the family and complains that everyone treats him like a baby. How can he see the situation in a way that he doesn't get upset?

For more information and empowering:

Check for updates, ideas for use of the book, and related products and programs at:

www.knock-kneedcowboy.com
www.empoweringforchange.com

Uncommon Horse Sense
(maybe not for the "tenderfoot")

Imagine a working cowboy walking into a city restaurant: Although his high-heeled boots with their clinking spurs and the bandana tied around his neck had their purposes and were standard dress in his world, today many people might consider both his dress—and him—"weird."

In all ages throughout history, groups of people have created their own costumes, traditions and customs. Some of these customs related to their idea of beauty; others, to what was "proper" or appropriate for the situation. This section is part investigation and part creative thinking.

1. In what two ways did the ancient Mayans make their babies especially beautiful?

2. Would the ancient Chinese have found Clementine attractive? Explain (Hint: You may have to find the children's or scout's version of the song.)

3. What do modern British judges and lawyers ("barristers") wear to court that their American equivalents do not?

4. Instead of using lipstick, explain how Ubangi people make their lips beautiful.

5. Find photos of both men and women's clothing from different eras in your own country, clothing (modern and past times) in other parts of the world, and/or from various cultures or religions. How might these different groups judge each other's choice of clothing?

6. Thinking about the result of your investigations above,

    a. What are some traditions, customs, or practices today that some people use to appear more attractive, better accepted, more intelligent, or envied?

    b. How might today's practices look to other cultures or times?

    c. Using your highly imaginative mind, create (draw or describe with words) a new tradition for another (future) generation. Explain why your creation will be so popular.

7. Describe one experience in which you (or someone you know) pre-judged another person (or people), but later found that the individual(s) were much like you. What did you learn through that experience?

Gracias, Pardner!

Deepest appreciation and love go to my husband Alan Jenkin and to my sons, Rusty and Trent Willmon These three men encourage me to celebrate my own uniqueness, never requiring that I act my age.

Rusty and Trent's dad, Ronald Dean Willmon, taught us about ranch life, guns, horses, and cattle. He also procured the original Troubles—a yapping fur ball that boldly defended against "fierce," grazing cattle the moment one of us stepped outside.

Special thanks to the staff and my co-authors of Wake Up Live and Wake Up Women. Their personal stories have inspired me to convert stumbling blocks to stepping stones.

Through Klemmer & Associates, many compassionate samurai—such as Rob Hubert, John Butruccio, and Kimberly Zink—have challenged me to "take on my life," refusing to permit me to play small. Thanks to my K&A teammate, Missy Beck-Lefaivre; her encouragement and statuesque beauty inspired the character Honey.

Another K&A teammate, Tricia Teague (author of *Football is Just Like Shopping*), proved that "getting off our 'orse" is a giant step toward any dream. She and the talented Patrick Gallagher (who designed and typeset this book) embody "the patience of Job."

Thanks to the fairy godfrog Gus, who reminds us to clarify what we really want in our lives.

With appreciation and celebration, BWJ

> "A man cannot be comfortable without his own approval."
>
> —Mark Twain

The Author

BILLIE WILLMON JENKIN says she began writing her first novel "when I was about eleven." During the following decades, though, her writing comprised personal letters, lesson plans, and speeches for her two ranch-raised sons. Eventually the retired teacher-turned-world-traveler began entertaining others with her travelogues doused with wit, humor, and insight for living.

Encouraged by friends, she began using her writing and life skills for wider audiences. She has recently co-authored two books in the best-selling "Wake-Up" series: *Wake Up... Live the Life You Love: Wake Up Moments I* and *Wake Up Women: BE Happy, Healthy, & Wealthy*. *The Knock-Kneed Cowboy: A Tale of Being "Just Right"...Just As We Are* is her first children's book.

Empowering others to make positive changes in their lives—while accepting "what is"—is the essence of Ms. Jenkin's life purpose.

"One must have the adventurous daring to accept oneself as a bundle of possibilities and undertake the most interesting game in the world, making the most of one's best."

—Harry Emerson Fosdick
American clergyman
1878–1969

Fans of
The Knock-Kneed Cowboy

What others are saying about...

The Knock-Kneed Cowboy: A Tale of Being "Just Right"...Just As We Are

"While *The Knock-Kneed Cowboy* is written as a children's book, it addresses the limiting belief of "I am not enough" that so many of us take on as children; and, if not dealt with and released, continues to negatively condition our experience of life as adults. I am delighted that Billie has chosen to make such a powerful contribution to the lives of both our children and ourselves."

—**Arlene Rannelli**
www.masteringyouressentialenergy.com
Facilitator of Human Potential

"This book is much more than an entertaining story. It is a true-to-the-heart experience about self-acceptance. My experiences as a psychotherapist have convinced me that liking oneself is the key to a healthy personality. I recommend this book as an ideal gift for any child whose happiness matters to you."

—**Gail Sherrill Phillips, MS, LPC, CCMHC**
Psychotherapist and author of *To Hold Her Head High*

"Both as chief of pediatrics in a clinic of five practitioners and in other children's services (such as three years work in a facility for incarcerated youth), I consider mental and emotional well-being vital to children's health.

"We know through research that a loving, accepting relationship (such as the character Honey has with her grandfather) confers resilience on children. While we've not yet developed an immunization against unhealthy emotions, the story relayed in this book (if taken to heart by both parents and children) provides a healthy dose of self-acceptance ... just what the doctor ordered! I heartily prescribe this book as a tonic for the emotional well-being for children of all ages!"

—**Sheila B Brown, MD, FAAP**
Pediatrician
Olympia, WA

"In a culture that places much stress on physical appearance, *The Knock-Kneed Cowboy* encourages readers—whether children or adults—to find satisfaction in who they are, exactly as they are. It is when we accept ourselves fully that we are most empowered to make the inward changes that we most want. A 'must-read.'"

—**Steven E**
Creator of the *Wake Up Live the Life You Love* series
Wakeuplive.com

"As an educator, former special education teacher and foster parent to a challenged child, I constantly have looked for materials and programs that support children's fragile self-esteem. *The Knock-Kneed Cowboy* is both an enjoyable tale and an excellent tool for parents and educators. Written by a retired teacher, this tale combines entertainment, opportunities for class discussion and creative writing, and expansion of reading skills. A "must-have" for teachers and parents of intermediate-grade students in any culture."

—**Kim Mason**
Educator of 20 years

A "Kids' Book" written for the entire family:

"This story is a parable that reflects everyone's life in some manner. Each of us struggles with our own acceptance; it's a journey most of us never actually finish. But it is in that acceptance of ourselves and others that we truly start to live. When we realize that our life's purpose is to give and empower others, the bitterness fades, and we start to be fruitful in ways we never thought possible when we were absorbed in our own insecurities."

—**Trent Willmon**
Country music recording artist
Author of *The Beer Man Cookbook*
www.trentwillmon.com

Check out our websites:

www.knock-kneedcowboy.com
www.empoweringforchange.com

Quick Order Form

Fax orders: (832) 213-1559

Telephone orders: Call (641) 715-3900 ext. 54218# (Secure Voicemail)

Email orders: *EmpoweringForChange@gmail.com*

Postal Orders: Empowering For Change, 213 Elkins Lake, TX 77340-7305 USA.
Telephone: (641) 715-3900, Ext. 54218#.

Please send ____ (quantity) copies of
"The Knock-Kneed Cowboy"
$17.95 per copy

Name: _____
Address: _____
City: _____
State: _____ **Zip:** _____
Telephone: _____
Email address: _____

Sales tax: Please add 8.25% for products shipped to Texas addresses.

Shipping:
U.S. $5.00 for first book, $3.00 for each additional book.
International: $8.00 for first book, $4.00 for each additional book.

Payment: ❏ Check
 ❏ Credit card:
  ❏ Visa ❏ MasterCard ❏ Discover

Card number: _____
Name on card: _____
Exp. Date: _____ V. Code: _____

Quick Order Form

Fax orders: (832) 213-1559

Telephone orders: Call (641) 715-3900 ext. 54218# (Secure Voicemail)

Email orders: *EmpoweringForChange@gmail.com*

Postal Orders: Empowering For Change, 213 Elkins Lake, TX 77340-7305 USA.
Telephone: (641) 715-3900, Ext. 54218#.

Please send ____ (quantity) copies of
"The Knock-Kneed Cowboy"
$17.95 per copy

Name: _____

Address: _____

City: _____

State: _____ **Zip:** _____

Telephone: _____

Email address: _____

Sales tax: Please add 8.25% for products shipped to Texas addresses.

Shipping:
U.S. $5.00 for first book, $3.00 for each additional book.
International: $8.00 for first book, $4.00 for each additional book.

Payment: ❏ Check
❏ Credit card:
❏ Visa   ❏ MasterCard   ❏ Discover

Card number: _____

Name on card: _____

Exp. Date: _____ V. Code: _____